Grim and Ghostly

STORIES

A Haunted Canada Book

**PAT HANCOCK
and ALLAN GOULD**

Illustrations by
Andrej Krystoforski

Revised edition. Originally published as
Ghosts and Other Scary Stories.

Scholastic Canada Ltd.

Toronto New York London Auckland Sydney
Mexico City New Delhi Hong Kong Buenos Aires

Scholastic Canada Ltd.
604 King Street West, Toronto, Ontario M5V 1E1, Canada
Scholastic Inc.
557 Broadway, New York, NY 10012, USA
Scholastic Australia Pty Limited
PO Box 579, Gosford, NSW 2250, Australia
Scholastic New Zealand Limited
Private Bag 94407, Greenmount, Auckland, New Zealand
Scholastic Ltd.
Villiers House, Clarendon Avenue, Leamington Spa,
Warwickshire CV32 5PR, UK

Library and Archives Canada Cataloguing in Publication
Hancock, Pat
Grim and ghostly stories : a haunted Canada book / Pat Hancock and
Allan Gould ; Andrej Krystoforski, illustrator.
Originally published: New York : Scholastic, 1993, under title: Ghosts and other scary
stories.
ISBN 0-439-94774-X
1. Children's stories, Canadian (English) 2. Horror tales, Canadian (English)
3. Ghost stories, Canadian (English) I. Gould, Allan, 1944- II. Krystoforski, Andrej, 1943-
III. Gould, Allan, 1944- Ghosts and other scary stories. IV. Title.

PS8565.A5695G75 2006   jC813'.54   C2006-900081-6

6 5 4 3 2 1   Printed in Canada   06 07 08 09 10

Contents

The Sleeping Boy

Something was wrong with the VCR. A young woman sitting near the front of the bus got up and fiddled with the buttons.

"It's the tracking. Adjust the tracking," somebody called from a few seats back. Impatiently, other passengers began to chip in their two cents' worth.

"Eject it and try again."

"About time they got DVD players on these tin cans."

"Keep it down, buddy. I'm trying to sleep. Why don't you do the same?"

"Cool it, will you? I'm trying, I'm trying," the young woman said.

Tempers were flaring. The driver knew he should do something. But at that moment, the VCR was the least of his worries. He was having trouble controlling the bus.

The passengers near the front were the first to

notice. Two men in the seats closest to the door began to nudge each other and whisper. A woman in the second row told the child beside her to sit up straight.

Gripping the steering wheel with one white-knuckled hand, the driver flipped on the loudspeaker with the other.

"May I have your attention, please?"

"Fix the movie."

"Shut up."

"Shhhhh, be quiet."

Finally the din faded to a low murmur and the driver tried again.

"Ladies and gentlemen, sorry about the movie, but right now we've got a bigger problem."

Although his heart was racing, he tried to look relaxed. He didn't want the passengers to sense how worried he was.

He took a deep breath and continued. "The engine seems to be losing a bit of power. Now, it's nothing to worry about. I just want you to know, that's all, so you won't be surprised if I have to pull over. If I do, would you kindly stay in your seats until I give you further instructions? And, uh, how about we just turn off the TVs for the moment?"

He pushed a button. The two screens went black. Then he leaned forward, focusing intently on the mountainous highway ahead. This was a difficult stretch of road — about thirty kilometres of twists, turns and steep grades before it linked up with the Trans-Canada. Definitely not a great place to run into problems.

At least the road was bare and dry. It had been two weeks since the last snow, and crews had long since finished sanding and plowing. Still, even under ideal conditions, a big vehicle like the bus needed full engine power to keep rolling. And right now, no matter how hard he pressed the accelerator, the bus was losing speed.

With dusk falling, the driver didn't want to be stranded at the side of a mountain highway with twenty cold, hungry, angry passengers. It might take hours to get a replacement bus. And that was assuming he could even get in touch with head office. For all he knew, the radio was on the fritz, just like the VCR.

He'd first noticed the trouble on the last long, steep grade. The bus had definitely lost power.

But what had really hardened the knot of fear that was forming in the pit of his stomach was the way the bus had headed into the oncoming lane — all on its own. In vain, he had wrestled with the steering wheel, trying to pull it back to the right.

He'd panicked briefly as they'd approached the crest of the hill. Was another bus, car or truck thundering to meet them head on?

Mercifully, the lane had been clear. But, as the bus coasted down the other side, still on the wrong side of the road, his fear grew.

He wasn't the only one who was scared. One of the two men in the front seats leaned over and asked quietly, "Are you having trouble with the steering?"

Before he could answer, an older woman farther back called out, "Driver, shouldn't we get out of the passing lane now?"

Other voices joined in.

"Come on, mister. Get over."

Once again, he flipped on the loudspeaker.

"Okay, folks, could we keep it down a bit, please? No point in getting everyone upset."

He paused until the bus was quiet, then went on.

"Look, I'm going to give it to you straight. I'm having a little trouble steering this baby. She's got a mind of her own at the moment. But we're still on the road, and we're obviously not speeding, so... Holy cow! Hold on!"

Without warning, the bus lurched forward, then fishtailed. For an agonizing moment, it slid sideways along the highway.

Finally, it came to rest, pointing directly at a snow-covered side road. Then it began to move again — straight up the narrow road.

Pandemonium broke out behind the driver.

Screams of fear filled the bus. A child started crying. Some adults did, too. One woman began to pray.

"I've had it," bellowed a man in a checked jacket. He picked his way up the aisle over the jumble of bags and coats that had spilled out of the overhead luggage compartments.

"Who do you think you are? Where'd you learn to drive?" he shouted when he reached the driver.

"Look, mister," the driver shouted back. "What do you see?"

He held his hands in the air as the steering wheel swung first to the right, then to the left, all on its own.

"And there?" he continued, pointing to his feet. They were planted firmly on the floor, not on the pedals. "I'm not driving this thing, buddy. I wish I were."

Horrified, the man backed up and fell into the doorwell. He pushed himself up and began to pound on the doors.

"Stop the bus! Let me out," he shrieked.

"Take it easy, fella. I'd stop if I could, believe me. I want out just as much as you do."

News of what was going on spread among the passengers like wildfire. Many of them began to shout and cry. The young woman who had tried to fix the VCR slipped out of her seat, crouched down on the top step, and began to talk quietly to the frantic man at the door. At the same time, the driver started talking over the PA system again.

"Please, everybody, stay in your seats," he pleaded, trying desperately to sound calm. The last thing he needed was a busload of hysterical passengers. He already had enough on his mind.

He cleared his throat and went on, "Look, I don't know what's happening any more than you do. The doors won't open. The steering wheel is useless, and so are the brake and accelerator. It seems somebody has us under remote control."

He swallowed hard, trying to control the quaver in his voice. "I'll keep doing what I can. But it would really help if you would try to stay calm. I know that's not easy. But if we panic, somebody is bound to be hurt. So far, nobody has been. And whoever — or whatever — is driving this bus is at least keeping us on the road. See? We're bouncing along nice and slow."

A fresh chorus of shrieks broke out as the bus swerved round a bend. It skittered off a pile of snow a plow had left at the roadside, then straightened out and went on.

Over the clamour, the driver tried to make a comforting joke.

"So, maybe he — or it — is new on the job, right?"

When nobody laughed, he continued. "Look, I know this road. We're on our way to Silver Lake — whether we like it or not. Someone will be there to give us a hand. Say, how about a little song? I bet the kids would like a song."

Clearing his throat, he began to sing in a deep voice.

"My eyes are dim, I cannot see…"

A few others joined in weakly.

"I have not got my specs with me…"

The chorus grew steadily louder until most of the passengers were singing nervously.

"I have not got my specs with me."

As they sang, the bus bounced forward jerkily, slithering on the bends but always clinging to the road.

An uneasy calm settled over the passengers. Most of them sat quietly, glancing out the windows or staring at the back of the seat ahead.

The driver had stopped trying to fight the nightmare. Still, he kept his hands lightly on the steering wheel and a foot poised over the brake pedal, just in case things returned to normal.

Suddenly, the bus rounded a bend and the village of Silver Lake lay ahead. A dozen or so low, wooden buildings lined its short main street. A ski lodge was nestled on a tree-lined slope above the village.

Between the trees in the distance, the setting sun reflected off the icy surface of a lake. It was a beautiful, peaceful scene except for one thing — the short street was jammed with traffic.

Some of the passengers began to clap while others gave a half-hearted cheer as the bus rolled slowly up the street, then came to an abrupt halt in front of a small general store. And there it stayed, right in the middle of the road.

"Now what?" the driver said to no one in particular. Outside, a crowd was gathering, waving to the passengers inside.

Cautiously, the driver reached for the lever that controlled the doors. He pulled it back, and was surprised to hear the familiar "whoosh" as the doors parted.

Gingerly, he tapped the horn. The loud honk startled the people in front of the bus. He grinned sheepishly and waved an apology. Then he stood and faced his passengers.

"Well, folks, I guess this is the end of the line. Let's see if we can find out what's going on."

As an afterthought, he started to add in his official voice, "And don't leave any valuables on the bus. Blueway is not responsible for..."

Before he could finish, people leaped from their seats and pushed past him. Like every good captain, he waited until the last passenger was safely off. Then he left, too.

The scene outside was confused. A truck driver

gestured wildly as he described his experience to the crowd.

"There we were, totally unable to do anything and…"

A woman in a turquoise ski suit interrupted.

"We were picked up. I swear it. My husband says I'm imagining things but, believe me, something picked up our van — the tan one over there — and moved it. Moved it right off the lane up to our chalet and onto the main road. Then it pushed us back into town, too."

"That's ridiculous," sneered the passenger in the checked coat. "You must have skidded on some ice. Made it seem as if you were airborne, that's all."

"The road was bare," the woman shot back huffily.

"You been drinking, lady?" another man asked.

A tall, grey-haired man stepped forward and said, "I haven't touched a drop in years, and the same thing happened to me and my wife. That's our Chevy over there."

The bus driver moved up beside him. "I wasn't drinking either. Mind you, we weren't picked up or anything. But we were…pushed. That's how it felt — as if something was pushing us around like a toy."

"This is crazy. I'm getting out of here," a voice shouted. Others joined in the chorus.

"Me, too."

"Yeah, come on. Let's go."

"Don't go — not yet."

The bus driver swung around. The last voice had come from behind him.

"Who said, 'Don't go'?" he asked.

"I did." An old man wearing a leather hat with fur earflaps jostled his way through the crowd. His grizzled beard rested on a wool scarf tucked inside the collar of his parka.

"Don't go yet," he pleaded. "It's not safe. Can't be. Otherwise he wouldn't have brought you here."

"Your brain's frozen, old man," one of the bus passengers yelled.

A woman pushed her way to the old man's side.

"Just a minute," she said firmly. "Don't you talk to Seth that way. He knows this area like the back of his hand. Show some respect. Now, Seth, what did you say?"

"He brought them here. Something's wrong somewhere and he brought them. Wait and see."

"Who's 'he'?" the driver asked.

"Yes, Seth. Who is 'he'?" the woman asked gently.

Silence had fallen over the crowd. Everyone was listening now, waiting to hear what the old man would say.

"The boy."

"What boy? Where?"

"The Sleeping Boy."

"The Sleeping Boy? Seth, what are you talking about?" Now even the woman was beginning to sound skeptical. "The only Sleeping Boy I know is the island in the lake."

"Yep, that's him," the old man nodded, clamping an old brown pipe between his teeth.

The woman turned to the driver and explained.

"There's a small island in the middle of the lake — beyond the trees, that way." She pointed into the darkness. "It's hard to see it now that the sun's gone down. Besides, it just looks like a huge lump of snow at the moment. The first settlers along the lake called it The Sleeping Boy because that's what it looks like from shore. The name stuck.

"People have been making up stories about it ever since. They say it's the body of a boy who got separated from his father when they went out to check their traplines. For days, he wandered, trying to keep warm at night by burrowing under the snow.

"One morning, he didn't wake up. When spring came and the snow melted, there he was, asleep in the middle of the lake. Legend has it that he lies there waiting for his father to find him and take him home."

The old man nodded as the woman talked. When she finished, he spoke again.

"True enough. But he wakes up sometimes."

"Oh, Seth. That's just a very old, very silly story," the woman said kindly.

Turning back to the driver, she continued, "There are some who say that the boy wakes up every now and then, just before something terrible is about to happen. They say he guards these hills, making sure no one comes to grief the way he did."

Another man pushed his way to the front of the crowd.

"Hogwash," he snorted. "I've lived here nearly as long as Seth and I don't believe a word of it. It's all rubbish."

He turned to face Seth and the woman.

"Why don't you tell them the one about how he wakes up every spring and pushes chunks of ice around on the lake like toy boats?" he asked sarcastically. "They say he's playing with them.

"Or how about the one that has him hanging around the animals — bears, badgers, groundhogs and the like. That's supposed to be why they wake up in spring — to play with him. Now that's a good one, don't you think?"

The crowd began to grow restless, laughing when a young man pointed at Seth and gestured that he was out of his mind.

"You're right there, fella," the man snickered.

Then he stomped over to the store, yanked open the door and disappeared inside.

"What about the forest fire?" Seth asked.

"Oh, Seth. That was just a coincidence," the woman said.

"Coincidence, you say? Not a cloud in the sky. People ready to move out because the fire was licking at the edge of town. And suddenly, a deluge. Right on the fire and nowhere else."

"Seth, that happened seventy years ago. People exaggerate over the years."

"Maybe so, but I was here then. Saw it myself with my own two eyes. And the train trestle. I was here then, too."

"What about the trestle?" the driver asked.

"Collapsed. Crashed right into the gorge. But the train — the one that was supposed to be on it right at that moment — was safe. The Boy stopped it, just short of the trestle. Then he pushed it back around the bend, all the way to the station. Nobody was hurt. The Boy made sure of that."

The woman looked confused.

"He's lost it," someone muttered.

The old man turned slowly until he was staring directly into the eyes of the speaker.

"Maybe so. Maybe so. But I wouldn't try to leave just yet if I were you. You're safe here. You'll see."

Then they heard it — a low distant rumble at first. It grew louder and louder until it erupted into a deafening roar. The ground vibrated under their feet.

"Avalanche!" someone screamed. People stood, open-mouthed, staring over the treetops as an enormous snowy-white cloud mushroomed into the darkening sky.

Finally, the roar faded to a faint echo. Still, the crowd stood in stunned silence.

The woman from the van found her voice. "That was over near our chalet," she said softly.

"And out by the highway," the bus driver added.

"Thanks, Boy," the old man said, looking up at the star-filled sky. He turned and began to walk away.

People cleared a path to let him pass. Then they, too, looked up at the sky — many offering their own silent thank you to The Sleeping Boy of Silver Lake.

Golden Eyes

Ashley had been speechless when her parents had given her a horse on her thirteenth birthday.

"For my very own?" she had finally sputtered, still thinking she must be dreaming.

"What are you going to call him?" her dad had asked.

"Sam," Ashley had answered quickly, certain that the strawberry roan would be a faithful companion, just like Frodo's Sam in *The Lord of the Rings*. "We'll go everywhere together!"

And go everywhere they did. Whenever she could, Ashley would saddle up Sam and head off with him to the places she'd been with her dad when she was learning to ride.

Once she had ridden Sam all the way to Duck Lake, and, another time, they'd gone as far as Dead Man's Hill. Today she was heading into the badlands for a close-up look at some hoodoos, fantastic pillars of layered rock that jutted out of the moon-like bar-rens.

It had taken major persuading to get her parents to let her go. They were nervous about her ranging so far from home.

"What if something goes wrong and you need help?" her mother had argued. "Hardly anybody lives out there."

"And those coulees can be pretty confusing. You could get turned around and never find your way out," her father had added.

Finally, though, they'd agreed. But only after Ashley had assured them that Sam never forgot the way back, and that she'd take extra food and water and a compass, just in case she got lost.

The sun was high overhead by the time Ashley and Sam reached the edge of the badlands. The grass had steadily grown patchier, and they'd spent the last ten minutes picking their way carefully across a couple of the barren coulees that had been gouged into the prairie landscape by retreating glaciers.

It was hot and Sam needed a rest. So did Ashley's rear end. A grove of spindly aspens clinging to the bank of an ancient, nearly dry creek offered the promise of a little shade and a drink for Sam.

Ashley tethered her horse so he could reach the trickle of water in the creek, took a sandwich out of her saddlebag, and sat down in the thin shade of one of the trees. Chewing slowly, she let her mind wander, imagining all sorts of exciting adventures that she and Sam might have out here in this weird, stark landscape.

Sam noticed the change in the weather first. His neighing snapped her out of her daydreams. She looked up. Sam was tossing his head to the right, then looking back at her. Off in the distance she saw what was worrying him. Thick black clouds were rolling in from the west and the fragile aspens were starting to sway in a strengthening breeze.

Ashley scrambled up, brushed herself off, and moved toward her horse.

"Good boy," she murmured, rubbing his velvety muzzle affectionately. Then she dug her jacket out of the saddlebag. "Just in case the weather changes," her mother would say whenever she checked to see if Ashley had it with her. The wind is really picking up, Ashley thought as she zipped it up. Seconds later, the sun disappeared behind the clouds and she heard the first distant rumble of thunder. A flash of sheet lightning followed.

Ashley scanned the threatening sky and made a face. There was no avoiding a good soaking — unless she could find shelter. Going farther west wasn't an option. She'd just be heading straight into the storm — and deeper into the badlands. Not much shelter there. Besides, she wanted to go home.

First, though, she had to get away from the trees. Whipped by fierce gusts of wind, they looked like they were about to snap and come crashing down. They also made perfect lightning rods.

She swung up onto Sam, checked her compass and nudged him back in the direction they'd come.

Sam maintained a steady pace, never faltering even when a blinding fork of lightning cut a jagged path to earth just ahead. Soon after, the first huge drops of rain splattered Ashley's jacket.

Ashley crammed her hat more tightly onto her head and hunkered down into her jacket. This didn't stop cold trickles of water from finding their way down her neck to her T-shirt.

She tried to guide Sam in the right direction but, eventually, she gave up. The rain had become so heavy that it was impossible to see more than a few metres ahead.

She'd have to trust Sam and simply hope that the two of them would stumble on help. She bent lower, hugged the horse's neck, and gave him his head.

Sam was picking his way slowly along what seemed to be the rocky bottom of a shallow coulee when Ashley thought she spotted something. She peered through the rain and waited for the next lightning flash to make sure. There it was again, off to the left

19

— the outline of a shed or shack.

"Come on, buddy," Ashley urged, reaching forward to pat Sam's neck. If anything, though, the horse began to slow down. Ashley dug in her heels and Sam kept going, but barely. As they neared the small building, he came to a dead stop. He wouldn't go any closer.

The rain eased a little, enough so that Ashley could make out more than an outline. Not much more, though, because there wasn't much more to see. Only two walls of what looked like a small house remained standing. Two walls and a chimney. The rest was a shell. Its charred, wet remains glistened in the murky light of the storm.

"No shelter here, Sam," Ashley said. "Let's get a move on."

Then she saw her, right in front of the burned-out cabin. She was tall and thin, and she seemed to be waving. Ashley rubbed the rain from her eyes and looked again. She was still there.

What's this girl doing way out here by herself? Ashley asked herself. Maybe she needs help, too. She kneed Sam forward, but the horse wouldn't budge.

It took some serious urging to get Sam moving. And then, when they got closer, he nearly bolted.

"Easy, boy, easy," Ashley soothed, grasping the reins firmly.

Now that she was close to the girl, she was glad that she'd decided to try to help. She looked about Ashley's age and she was eerily pale. Her long, dark hair was plastered against her cheeks, and her clothes — a yellow shirt and jeans — were dripping wet. But it was her eyes that made the most impact. Even in the poor light, Ashley could see that they were golden.

She'd never met anyone with golden eyes before. What's more, when the girl looked at her, Ashley felt as if those eyes could see right through her.

"Are you okay?" Ashley began nervously. She couldn't think of anything else to say.

The stranger nodded and reached out.

"You want a ride?"

Again, she nodded.

Her response was accompanied by another rumble of thunder, farther away this time. Still, she reacted with a jolt, her eyes filling with fear.

"Okay, hop on," Ashley said, holding out her hand. The thin girl grabbed it and Ashley pulled her up behind. She didn't have to worry about Sam handling the extra weight. The girl was amazingly light, wet clothes and all. Still, Ashley thought she felt Sam tremble a little as she settled in.

Now what? she thought. I'm not sure how to get out of here and, if *she* knows, she's not saying.

As if reading Ashley's mind, the girl tapped her

arm and pointed to the right. Squinting through the rain, Ashley thought she could make out a narrow track winding upwards out of the coulee.

"You want me to go that way?"

She felt the bent head nod against her shoulder.

"Okay, you don't have to talk, but I'm Ashley Robbins. Just so you know. Hold on."

Sam needed little prompting this time, moving toward the track as soon as Ashley flicked the reins.

Gradually, the rain wound down to a fine drizzle until, finally, it stopped altogether. Then the setting sun broke through the clouds behind them, casting a fiery glow on the drenched countryside.

"Red sky at night, sailor's delight," Ashley said, feeling a little foolish as she tried once more to make conversation. "At least I know now we're heading east. I live east of here. Is that where you live, too?" Again, all she felt was a slight nod against her shoulder. That, and the soft breathing on the back of her neck. That was no comfort. If anything, it sent shivers down her spine.

Now that she was starting to dry off a little, Ashley realized it was the strange girl's breath, not the evening air, that was chillingly cold. The realization sent a wave of goosebumps spreading across Ashley's damp shoulders and down her back.

She resisted the urge to turn up the collar of her

jacket. She didn't want to upset her mysterious passenger. The whole situation was weird enough already. All she wanted was to get to the girl's house — or wherever they were going — and call home.

Home. Just the thought of it warmed Ashley up a little. Home, and fried eggs and bacon and hash browns. Home, and a soft bed and a cozy quilt. Home, home. Home, home. Her head began to bob in time to the rhythm of Sam's hooves. The last thing she remembered before dozing off was a thin, cold hand moving over hers to grab the reins as they slipped from her grasp.

Later, much later, she awoke to the crunching of gravel and the on-off flashing of a spinning red light. Sam was standing quietly on the shoulder of a paved road and, incredibly, Ashley was still in the saddle.

"Is that you, Ashley?" a voice called. She turned toward it, but was blinded by the headlights of a car. Two strong, warm hands reached up to help her out of the saddle.

"Officer Kovalski," she whispered hoarsely, as her eyes adjusted to the light. "Boy, am I glad to see you."

"Me too, but now we've got to get you home," Kovalski said. "This is Cal's place. Tether your horse to his gate. I'll call and get him to put it in the barn for the night. Your folks can bring the trailer and pick it up in the morning."

"My folks!" Ashley was suddenly frantic. "I have to call them."

"Take it easy, girl," Kovalski gave Sam's reins a tug to make sure she had tied them securely to the fence. "I'll radio in and the dispatcher will call them. They're pretty worried. That freak storm caused a slew of flash floods out in the badlands — and they told us that's where you were headed. The sergeant and Bill are out there now in the four-by-four looking for you."

"Sorry," Ashley mumbled. "I didn't know a storm could come up that fast."

"No harm done," Kovalski said as he opened the door and guided her into the passenger seat of the cruiser.

"Wait!" Ashley suddenly remembered the girl. "Where is she?"

"Who?"

"The girl that was riding with me — the one who showed me the way back."

"No girl around when I found you," Kovalski said, slamming the door.

"Then you'll have to look for her, too," Ashley said. "What if she slipped off after I fell asleep? I can't believe I did that. I just couldn't keep my eyes open."

"There was no sign of any girl, and we've had no

missing-person reports — other than you, of course," Kovalski said as he slipped into the driver's seat and started the engine. "No harm, though, in taking a drive down the road to see what we can find. What did she look like?"

"Well, she was about my age, maybe a little younger. And she had long brown hair and golden eyes."

Kovalski stiffened and turned to stare at Ashley. "Golden eyes? What else?"

"Well, she was really skinny and she was wearing a yellow top and jeans. And she was just standing there in the pouring rain in the middle of nowhere. Well, sort of in the middle of nowhere. There was an old cabin, but it looked like it had burned down. All that was left was a chimney and parts of a couple of walls. Why? Do you know her?"

Kovalski looked puzzled, "About your age, right? You're sure?"

"Maybe a little younger. Why?" Ashley repeated.

"Oh, the golden eyes…" Kovalski hesitated. "Reminded me of Sarah Jackson. But that's an old case. Happened at least ten years ago. She'd be in her twenties by now — if she survived — so it couldn't have been her. The eyes threw me for a minute. I'd never heard of anyone with golden eyes before Sarah — and, come to think of it, I haven't since."

"What happened?" Ashley was almost afraid to ask.

"She disappeared. Took off into the badlands one day. In fact, there was a flash flood that day, too. After it was over, we searched — but never found any trace of her. These sudden floods can be pretty vicious, the way they come barrelling down the coulees without any warning. We figure she got swept away. Her bones are probably still out there somewhere."

Ashley's stomach tightened. She sat quietly as they drove, scarcely breathing as the meaning of Kovalski's words sank in.

"Her parents moved to High River after that," Kovalski continued. "Ended up leaving their place empty. Nobody was interested in buying it. Pretty unfriendly country there, right on the edge of the badlands. It burned down a few years later."

Kovalski looked at Ashley and shrugged. "End of story."

He reached for the radio and clicked the microphone. "I better call the Sarge and Bill. They've been out there for hours."

As the radio crackled to life, Ashley sat stunned, shivering despite the warm air blasting out of the heater.

"Listen, Bill, I've got the Robbins kid. Found her safe and sound on the road by Cal's place."

"That's good news. Sarge and I will go on in then."

"Catch you back at the station. How's it looking out there, anyway? Much damage?"

"Nah," Ashley heard Bill respond through the static. "Near as we can tell the only damage was to the ruins of the old Jackson property. And that's no great loss. Looks like the flood swept right through the place and took out everything in its path. There isn't a bush or tree in sight and the ruins are gone. Totally. Good thing the Robbins kid wasn't out here, after all, or she'd be gone, too."

Payback

Michael Smithson took a last look at the cover page of his Not-So-Famous Inventors project. It's great, he thought, even if I do say so myself.

But Michael knew he couldn't take all the credit. The new printer his mom had bought for her home office had helped — a lot. Good thing she'd let him use it.

"Remember, Michael," she'd warned as she was leaving, "my computer's not a toy. It's part of my business. If anything goes wrong, just leave things alone and wait for me. I'll be back around 5:30."

Nothing had gone wrong. Carefully, Michael placed the pages in the dark blue folder his mom had given him and reached for his bag.

Better pack it right now so I don't forget, he thought. That's when he spotted the note his friend had given him. Dave was in grade eight and he was a real computer freak.

Michael stared at the slip of paper.

"You've got high speed, right?" Dave had said, scribbling something. "So go to this website. It's got all kinds of games you can play. You can download them, too, instead of buying them."

Michael could hear his mother's voice. She hated anything that was pirated. "It's immoral," she would say, "and probably illegal too."

But Dave had said the games were really amazing. No one will know if I just take a little peek, Michael reasoned. He sat back down at the desk. With two clicks of the mouse he was ready. He took another look at the website on the note, hesitated briefly, then typed it into the address box. Then he clicked on the Go arrow and waited.

The opening screen was fantastic. Flames rose and burned their way through the title graphics of the website's home page, Infinity Zone. Then the screen filled with a purple mist and eerie music began to play as a ghostly hand wiped the screen clear.

Now we're in business, Michael thought. Mom'll never know if I just play for a little while.

The site's main menu popped up on the left, and Michael clicked on Games. Then he scanned the list of choices. He recognized some of the names, but not many. GETAWAY sounds good, he thought. Clicking on it, he waited for the game to load.

Nothing happened. Finally, a Please Wait message began flashing on and off in the top corner of the screen. Michael waited. Still nothing.

Okay, I've waited, I've waited, he thought. This is stupid. Something must be wrong. I'll try another game. Just as he was about to click the Back button, the screen colour changed to bright yellow. Black letters began to appear, one at a time, as if someone were typing them.

DON'T DO THAT, MICHAEL.

Startled, Michael let go of the mouse.

GOOD. CLICKING ON THE BACK BUTTON WILL SILENCE ME.

This is really strange, Michael thought. He hadn't entered his name. Yet there it was — Michael. And how could it know what I was about to do, he wondered.

More letters began to appear.

I NEED TO TALK TO YOU.

This is too weird, Michael thought. Slowly he slid the mouse upwards, hoping to click on the small X in the top right corner and close the window that way. But the arrow froze, and again large letters flashed across the screen.

I SAID DON'T DO THAT.

Michael felt as if someone had just shouted at him. Stunned, he stared at the monitor, trying to figure out what to do next. Suddenly, a blinking cursor appeared near the bottom of the screen. All right, here goes nothing, he thought, and tapped the W key. A W appeared on the screen. Michael kept typing.

WHAT DO YOU WANT?

VERY GOOD. INTERACTION AT LAST. YOU WILL HELP ME. PLEASE WAIT.

Michael waited while the hard drive whirred. Then a new message appeared.

THANK YOU. MODIFICATIONS ARE COMPLETE. NO NEED TO TYPE NOW. YOU CAN TALK TO ME.

Puzzled, Michael typed again.

YOU MEAN TALK, LIKE WITH MY VOICE?

YES.

Michael listened for footsteps downstairs, making sure his mother hadn't come back early. Then he said softly, "Okay. I'm talking."

GOOD. THE MODIFICATIONS WERE SUCCESSFUL. PLEASE SPEAK UP A LITTLE.

"Okay, I'm speaking up. Now what?" Michael asked nervously.

WILL YOU HELP ME, MICHAEL?

There's my name again, Michael thought. I can't believe this. I'm talking to a computer game. Aloud, he asked, "How do you know my name?"

I KNOW MANY THINGS NOW THAT I AM

Michael waited. Nothing more appeared. "Now that you're what?" he finally blurted out.

DEAD.

"Dead?" Michael repeated. "Are you serious? What kind of sick mind came up with this game?"

BELIEVE ME, THIS IS NO GAME.

"What is it, then?"

A PLEA FOR HELP. I NEED YOU. NOW THAT I'M NOT ALIVE.

"Sure, and I'm not sitting at this desk either."

WRONG. YOU REALLY ARE THERE. I AM NOT.

"You mean you're a ghost?" Michael asked.

YES.

One word, there on the screen — YES. It wasn't the answer he'd expected.

"You're telling me that you're a ghost...that there's a ghost in my mom's computer?"

YES. I DO NOT HAVE A BODY. I CANNOT MAKE MYSELF HEARD. THAT IS WHY I NEED YOU.

Michael felt the hairs on the back of his neck stand up, just like they did when he was alone in the house after dark and imagined a burglar was trying to break in.

"Me? You need me? No way. This is stupid," Michael said. He hit Escape, expecting the screen to go blank. Instead more typing appeared.

YOU CANNOT DO THAT.

"That's what you think," Michael said grimly. "No stupid game is going to tell me what to do."

He pressed the computer's power button. It didn't respond.

This can't be happening, Michael thought, reaching behind the computer. He grabbed the plug and tried to pull it out of the power bar. It wouldn't budge.

YOU CANNOT DO THAT, EITHER.

34

Oh, no, he thought. How am I going to explain this to Mom? He turned back to the screen, where another message was appearing.

YOU CANNOT SILENCE ME. YOU MUST HELP ME. THEN I WILL GO.

"How?" pleaded Michael. "Just tell me what I have to do to end this."

I NEED YOU TO GET A MESSAGE TO MY GIRLFRIEND.

Still hoping against hope that this really was some sort of weird game, Michael said, "So do it yourself. You're the one with all the power, not me. I haven't had a chance to win any powers yet."

I REPEAT. THIS IS NOT A GAME AND I AM NOT THAT POWERFUL. I AM TRAPPED IN THIS NETWORK. POSTING GETAWAY ONLINE TODAY WAS MY LAST CHANCE. THEN I HAD TO WAIT FOR SOMEONE LIKE YOU TO CHOOSE IT.

"All right, you win," Michael said flatly. "What do I have to do?"

YOU HAVE TO CALL HER.

"Call her? Why?"

I WORK - I USED TO WORK - AT THE STOCK EXCHANGE. ANOTHER GUY AND I WERE BYPASSING SECURITY CODES AND DEPOSITING MONEY INTO A BOGUS ACCOUNT.

The words were appearing very quickly now, as fast as someone could say them.

YESTERDAY THE EXCHANGE ANNOUNCED PLANS TO INSTALL NEW SECURITY SOFT-WARE, AND DIRK AND I KNEW WE'D GET CAUGHT. SO I TRANSFERRED THE MONEY - NEARLY $7 MILLION - TO TWO ACCOUNTS AT A BANK IN THE CAYMAN ISLANDS - ONE FOR DIRK AND ONE FOR ME. A 50-50 SPLIT.

The screen suddenly went blank, and Michael took a deep breath. Just the thought that he might actually be talking to a dead criminal was making his heart race. Then the words started again.

LAST NIGHT I WENT TO MY GIRLFRIEND'S PLACE TO TELL HER WHAT WE'D DONE. I HID MY NEW ACCOUNT'S PASSWORD NUMBER THERE. THEN I ASKED HER TO LEAVE THE COUNTRY WITH ME. I TOLD HER WE COULD SPEND THE REST OF OUR DAYS LIVING IN A TROPICAL PARADISE.

"What did she say?" Michael couldn't resist asking.

SHE WASN'T SURE. SHE ASKED FOR TIME
TO THINK. SO I SAID I'D CALL TODAY.
IF SHE SAID YES, I WAS GOING TO TELL
HER ABOUT THE PASSWORD AND SHE COULD
BRING IT TO THE AIRPORT FOR THE
FLIGHT TO THE CAYMANS.

"But you're...dead. This isn't going to happen because you're dead." Michael couldn't believe he had just said that.

YES. DIRK PICKED ME UP EARLY THIS MOR-
NING TO GO AND HIDE OUT NEAR WINKLER'S
COVE FOR THE DAY. WE WERE NEARLY THERE
WHEN WE SUDDENLY SWERVED OFF THE
ROAD AND CRASHED INTO THE ROCK FACE.
THE PAIN WAS HORRIBLE. THE LAST
THING I REMEMBER WAS DIRK PUSHING
OPEN HIS DOOR.

Now Michael really was scared. Before his mom had left for work she had the radio on, and he had heard that traffic had been backed up for hours because of a fatal accident on the coast road. The car had caught fire and exploded. The police reported finding evidence of one body, but couldn't confirm yet if there were more.

"That was you? Is Dirk dead, too?"

I DON'T KNOW YET. NOW YOU HAVE TO
CALL MY GIRLFRIEND. TELL HER WHERE I
HID THE PASSWORD. ASK HER TO GIVE IT
TO THE POLICE. I WANT TO RETURN MY
SHARE OF THE MONEY.

"But I'm just a kid. She'll hang up on me. Maybe I can get someone else to help you."

NOBODY ELSE WILL BELIEVE YOU.

Michael thought for a moment, trying to imagine explaining this to his mother — or Dave — or anybody.

"I know," he whispered. "Even I don't believe this."

SO YOU HAVE TO DO IT RIGHT NOW. OR
YOUR MOTHER'S COMPUTER WILL CRASH.

"Okay, okay," Michael sputtered. "What's her number? And her name. Don't forget her name. And yours? I'll need to know that, too."

CORRINE BELIVEAU. 555-9993. I AM -
WAS - GRAHAM.

Michael's hands shook as he reached for the phone on the table nearby and pressed the numbers.

After five rings a woman finally answered.

"Hello?"

"Uh, er, hello?" he said, trying to make his voice sound deeper. He moved the receiver closer to the computer, too. Just in case it could hear, he thought. Then he went on.

"May I please speak to Corrine Beliveau?"

"Speaking."

"Uh, you don't know me or anything, but Graham wants me to give you a message."

"…Graham?" The woman on the other end of the line choked out the name.

"Yes, Graham."

"He has a message for me? What are you talking about? He's… Never mind. Who are you?" the woman asked, sounding alarmed.

"Graham wants to return the money," Michael blurted, forgetting to change his voice.

"What…? Hey, you're just a kid. What's going on?" Now the woman sounded angry.

"He wants you to give his bank account password to the police," Michael continued. "He hid it at your place."

"He did, did he? Then where is it?"

Michael realized he didn't know where it was. He covered the mouthpiece, and whispered, "Where is it?"

UNDER THE BLUE LAMP ON THE END TABLE.

Michael repeated the words as they appeared on the screen.

"How do you know I have a blue lamp? Are you stalking me or something? I'm going to hang up."

"No, no," Michael pleaded. "Please don't do that. Go look, just in case he's…" Michael stopped in mid-sentence, realizing he would sound crazier than he already did if he said any more.

"I don't know why I'm doing this," the woman said. Michael heard her put down the receiver and walk away. He waited for more than a minute. At one point he thought he heard some muffled whispers in the background. Then he heard footsteps again.

Thank goodness she's coming back, he thought.

"Tell your Graham there's nothing there."

Michael heard a sharp click, and the line went dead.

"Hello? Hello?" he repeated. "She's gone! Do I have to call her back?" Michael asked, looking at the screen.

NO. I KNOW NOW WHAT SHE IS. AND I KNOW WHAT SHE WILL DO.

The words were coming slowly again.

THERE   MUST BE   ONE MORE   CALL.

"No," Michael whimpered. "Please don't make me. Go away. My mom will be home soon."

FIGURED OUT   TO DO   MYSELF.

Words seemed to be missing now.

MUST   SAVE   POWER.   GOOD B

Michael waited nervously, but no more text appeared on the monitor. Suddenly the message Press Any Key to Continue popped up. He hit the space bar and the normal screen was back. He returned to the menu and called up Games. Quickly, he scanned the listings. GETAWAY wasn't there.

This is crazy, Michael thought. Then he glanced at his watch. His mother was due home any minute. Frantically, he hit Start, then clicked on Turn Off Computer. Please let me get out of this, he thought, watching the screen anxiously. After a few seconds, the computer shut down.

Michael grabbed the note from Dave with the website on it, ripped it up and threw the pieces into the wastebasket. Then he grabbed his bag, turned off the lights in the office, and ran downstairs.

He flopped on the couch. His head was reeling and he was feeling more than a little shaky.

"No one will believe me. I've got to forget this," he said out loud. He shook his head. "And I've got to stop talking to myself, too."

This didn't happen, this didn't happen, he repeat-ed silently, as he reached for the TV remote. When his mom arrived home a few minutes later, she found him watching the final minutes of a junior hockey game.

Michael didn't say anything to his mom about what had happened. And the next day at school when Dave asked him about the games, he muttered some-thing about trying one and not liking it, then quickly changed the subject. For the next few days he tried to push the whole experience to the back of his mind. But he was nervous every time he turned on the com-puter.

On Friday he heard the news.

He was eating breakfast with his mom and, as usual, the radio was playing in the background. Michael nearly choked on a mouthful of oatmeal when he heard the news lead off with, "At a press conference last night police announced the arrest of Dirk Malvoy and Corrine Beliveau."

"Are you OK, Michael?" his mother asked.

"Shhhh," he insisted, listening intently.

"Acting on an anonymous tip, detectives picked up the pair for questioning as they were about to board a flight to the Cayman Islands. When dental records confirmed the identity of the body found in a burned-out car on the coast road as that of Graham Carver, Malvoy was charged with his murder, and Beliveau as an accessory. Police are still investigating their links to Carver and to a possible computer crime involving the theft of millions of dollars from the stock exchange."

Michael's mom switched off the radio and reached over to touch his forehead.

"Are you feeling sick?" she asked, sounding worried. "You're as pale as a ghost."

Just hearing that word made Michael tremble. He managed to get his books together and convince his mother that he was fine to go to school.

But as he walked toward the bus stop his mind was still reeling. Did the ghost do this? Did he figure out how to contact the police before he lost all his power?

But why? he wondered as he watched the bus approach. What did he tell them?

He was still trying to untangle that mystery when the bus pulled up. Once on, he slid into an empty seat near the front, wanting time to think. But Dave came forward from the back and plunked down beside him.

"So, are you ready for the French test?"

"I hope so," Michael answered. Then it hit him. Test. The ghost had been testing his girlfriend. He must have suspected she was part of a double-cross. Dirk's double-cross.

She had seemed annoyed when I said I had a message from him, Michael thought. She didn't ask me where he was or anything. I bet she never gave that password to the police. She and Dirk wanted all the money. That's got to be it, he told himself. It was a test. And Corrine had failed.

Michael shifted uneasily in his seat, thinking how close he had been to corruption and murder — and to a ghost and his revenge. He shivered as the bus pulled up in front of the school, relieved that he had escaped unharmed. But it's over now, he thought, and all I have to worry about is my French test. It's over. It has to be...

Game Boy

Like every other Game Boy owner, Steve Filmore ate, drank, slept and lived video games. He spent every spare second with his new system. So it came as no surprise when his math test came back with a big red 43 at the top.

The night before, when he was supposed to be studying, Steve decided to try just one game. One game led to another...and another...and, suddenly, it was time for bed. The evening had disappeared, swallowed up by the electronic monster.

Now what? he wondered, as he crossed the schoolyard. Mr. Harper had kept him in for "a little chat" about his test result, so the playground was nearly empty. Just as well, too. Steve was in no mood to talk to anybody.

He headed out to the lone tree at the edge of the baseball diamond and flopped down against the trunk. Lately, he'd been hiding out there a lot. It was a great place for playing video games. No one bugged him.

Steve reached into his backpack and dug under his math book to find his Game Boy. Within minutes, he was lost in a Super Mario adventure. An entire baseball team could have thundered past and he wouldn't have noticed.

So when the voice broke his concentration, he nearly jumped out of his skin. He hadn't heard anyone coming.

Steve stared at the boy who was crouched beside him looking intently at the Game Boy screen. He was definitely a kid, yet his face had the wizened, wrinkled look of an old man.

"What did you say?" Steve asked, tearing his eyes away from the strange-looking face.

"I said, do you have to jump on all those guys?"

"Oh yeah. You have to. You get more points."

"Is it hard?"

"Uh, not once you get the hang of it. After that, the more you play, the better you get."

"I get it. Like math," the boy said, pointing to the textbook.

Steve stared again. This kid doesn't just look old, he thinks old, too, he thought. He must be the only kid on earth who thinks video games are like math.

"No way," Steve said aloud. "This is nothing like math. This is fun."

"I always thought math was fun."

"You're nuts. It sucks."

As Steve spoke, he popped out the game and replaced it with the *Tetris* cartridge.

"What's your name?" he asked as he began to play again.

"Ben."

"Ben who?"

"Ben Farber. What's yours?"

"Stephen Filmore. But call me Steve. Only my mom calls me Stephen."

"I know what you mean. Mine used to call me Benjamin."

"But she doesn't anymore? How'd you get her to stop?"

"Um...she just stopped, that's all. You know, you're really lucky to have a game like this. It looks amazing."

"It is. I don't remember seeing you around here before. Are you new?"

"No. I've seen you before, though."

"Oh, but you don't go to this school, right?"

"No, I don't go to this school."

Steve was really concentrating now. The shapes were falling fast and he had to slot them into place quickly. He didn't hear what Ben said next.

"Sorry. What did you say?"

"I asked if you'd let me have a turn sometime," Ben said shyly.

Steve glanced at his watch.

"Oops," he said. "Not today, that's for sure. I've got to get home." He shut off the game and began to pack up. "Besides, in another week, I probably won't be playing it myself."

"What do you mean?" Ben asked.

"Well, Mr. Harper — my math teacher — says he'll tell my folks if I flunk another test."

"But what does that have to do with your game?"

"Are you kidding? If my mom and dad find out I'm flunking tests, they'll take it away. They said they would, and they meant it."

"Oh." Ben frowned, then his face brightened. "Hey, I've got an idea. Suppose you pass your next test…"

"Get serious."

"Well, just suppose you do. Then you'd have your game for a while longer at least, right?"

"Yeah. Until I flunk the test after that, anyway."

"But you won't flunk another test. Not if you practise. Math is just like playing video games, really. Once you get the hang of it, you just have to practise to get better. I was pretty good at math. What grade are you in?"

"Six."

"That's good. I got past that," Ben said.

I would hope so, Steve thought. He looks old enough to be a professor or something. Just really small for his age.

Ben continued, "When's your next test?"

"Monday."

"Okay. How about this? I help you with your math for the rest of the week. If you do better on the next test, you let me use your Game Boy for just one night. What do you think?"

"A whole night?" Steve couldn't imagine lending out his Game Boy for more than five minutes.

"Well, if you don't do well, you might lose it forever. And I would really love to play some of those games, especially that last one — *Tetris*. They weren't around when I...I mean, where I lived."

"No way. Where were you? On the moon or something?"

"Something like that. Now, what do you say? Is it a deal?"

Steve hesitated, then shrugged. "Okay. What do we do? You wanna come to my house or do you want me to go to yours?"

"Oh..." Ben seemed confused. "How about we meet right here after school every day? Behind this tree? You're the only one who ever comes here, and..."

"How do you know that?" Steve interrupted

sharply. Maybe this wasn't such a good idea after all, he thought. I don't even know this kid. And from the sound of it, he's been watching me.

"Oh…uh…I've seen you here a few times, that's all. I don't go to school here, but I wish I could."

"Well, why can't you?"

Again, Ben seemed confused. Then he went on.

"Well, my mom and dad had to move here. And the school year had already started, so Mom decided to teach me at home." He paused, as if remembering something, then added, "She used to be a teacher. That's what I wanted to be, too."

"Wow, no school! That would be great."

"It wasn't…isn't. It's actually pretty boring."

"Yeah, I guess so," Steve said. "I never thought about that."

"So," Ben said suddenly. "About this math. You've got your books with you. Why don't we start right now?"

"Okay," Steve said reluctantly. "But this is a waste of time. You'll see."

An hour later, he wasn't so sure. Ben was patient and he had a way of coming up with great examples. Decimals were parts of his allowance and fractions were parts of *Tetris* scores. Steve was surprised when he checked his watch and saw that it was nearly dinnertime.

"I've really got to go," he said, packing his bag.

"Same time tomorrow, then?" Ben suggested hopefully.

"No problem, it's your time that we're wasting," Steve said as he took off across the yard. At the gate, he turned back and shouted, "Hey, thanks," but Ben was nowhere in sight.

The next afternoon, Steve had to help set up chairs for a PTA meeting. It was nearly four o'clock when he headed for the old tree, hoping Ben would still be there.

It wasn't until he got right up to the tree and peeked around the trunk that he saw him. Ben was sitting with his hands clasped around his knees, staring at some kids playing Frisbee in the park across the street.

"Hi, Steve," he said without looking up. Then he turned and smiled. "So, our deal is still on?"

"Guess so. But you're the one who's gonna lose out, Ben."

"Let's just see what happens," Ben smiled.

Once more, he helped Steve work through the world of multiplication, division, numerators and denominators.

They met again on Wednesday and Thursday. By Friday, Steve was beginning to think that doing well on a math test just might be more than a dream.

"See," Ben said as they finished up, "it's really not

so bad after all, is it?"

Grudgingly, Steve agreed that it wasn't as hard as he'd thought.

"But," Ben warned, "you should try those last questions one more time over the weekend. Don't look at the answers in the back until you're finished. The test is Monday morning, right? When will you get it back?"

"Actually, Mr. Harper said he'd mark mine right away. If I bomb, which I probably will, he said he'll be on the phone to my parents Monday night."

"No way that's gonna happen. You know your stuff now. And I can have your Game Boy Monday night?"

"Sure. A deal's a deal. I'll give it to you Monday after school. But just for one night."

"One night," Ben said, beaming. "That's all."

The happy look on Ben's face gave Steve an idea.

"Hey," he said as he packed up his books, "we always have tacos on Friday night. You wanna come to my place for dinner? My folks won't mind. There's always lots, and..."

He stopped. Ben's smile had disappeared and, for a moment, it looked like he was about to cry. Then he said lightly, "Nah, but thanks for asking. And don't worry about Monday. You'll ace it, Steve. I know it."

"Sure," Steve said sarcastically. "See ya," he called

as he began to jog toward Park Street.

"Goodbye, Steve," Ben said quietly.

"What did you say?" Steve shouted.

"I said good luck," Ben yelled back.

"Thanks," Steve hollered. "I'll need it."

He spent much of the weekend doing homework — not just math, but social studies and English, too. He couldn't believe how much catching up he had to do.

After dinner on Sunday, he went back to his math. When he was unsure about one question — the last and the hardest — he went downstairs to ask for help. His parents were in the living room.

"Hey, could one of you help me with this?" He sat down on the couch and showed them the question.

His dad began to scribble numbers.

"Dad, could you write the percents as fractions of a hundred right at the beginning? That's the way Ben showed me. I can follow it easier."

"Who's Ben?" Mom asked.

"He's just this kid who's been helping me with my math."

"I don't remember you mentioning a Benjamin before."

"Ben, Mom, Ben. And I haven't. He's just this kid I met after school."

"Really? What's his last name? How old is he? And

where does he live? Does he go to your school?"

Steve could tell that his mother's Beware of Strangers warning system had just clicked into action.

"Mom, it's fine. He's just a kid, and he's really smart, too. His name is Farber — Ben Farber. He doesn't go to my school — and I never asked him how old he was because I didn't want to hurt his feelings."

"What do you mean?" Dad asked. He'd stopped writing and was listening carefully now, too.

"Well, he's a little shorter than me and he acts like a kid, but he looks kind of old. It's hard to explain."

"What did you say his name was?" Dad asked, looking alarmed.

"Ben Farber."

"You shouldn't joke about Ben," his mother said, pursing her lips. "Besides, how did you hear about him?"

"Mom, what's with you? I'm not joking."

"Okay, then. Did you just make up this story about getting help to impress us? So we won't take the Game Boy away or something?"

Steve was confused. It looked like he was in trouble — and he had no idea why.

"He could have just lucked into the name," Dad said to Mom over Steve's head.

"Yes, but what about what he said about the way he looked?" his mother asked nervously.

"Hey guys, I'm here. Talk to me. What's this all about? Ben's just a kid I met, I tell you. And he just looks a lot older than a kid. A few wrinkles like Granddad, that's all."

"We're being ridiculous," Dad said abruptly. "Let's get back to this problem."

"No, wait." Steve wasn't willing to let it drop. Something strange was happening. "What's wrong?"

"It's nothing, really," Mom said. "It's just that there was a boy named Benjamin Farber who moved here when we were kids. His family wanted to be closer to the medical centre. Ben needed so much special care by then."

"By when? What was wrong with him?"

"Well, we never met him. But our parents told us about him."

"Yes," Dad continued. "He had a very serious — and very rare — disease, one that makes your body grow old in just a few years."

"By the time they moved here, Ben was already too weak to go to school. And apparently he really wanted to. He was just a kid. He wanted to do all the things other kids did."

"He died about six months after they arrived," Mom added. "It was so sad. His parents moved away soon after the funeral. So you can see why we were so surprised by what you said, can't you?"

Steve was stunned. This is crazy, he thought.

"Forget it," Dad said. "It's just a coincidence, that's all. Now let's get back to this problem, shall we?"

Steve sat quietly while Dad finished explaining the math question, but he wasn't paying much attention. As soon as possible, he escaped to his room.

There has to be an explanation, he thought, as he slipped into bed. There just has to be.

By the time he got to school the next morning, he'd convinced himself that Dad was right — it was all just a coincidence.

Steve was surprised when he was one of the first to finish the math test. He was also surprised to find that he'd at least tried every question. A first. Once the test was over, though, the rest of the day seemed to drag endlessly.

When Mr. Harper finally dismissed the class, he asked Steve to stay behind. Steve's heart was pounding as he waited to hear his fate.

"How did you do it, Steve? Congratulations." Mr. Harper handed him his paper. At the top, with a big happy face beside it, was a large blue 81.

"I think you've finally got the basics, Steve. You keep this up and your mark will be much better on your next report."

Steve thanked Mr. Harper and left in a daze. He

wandered slowly out to the schoolyard, where he stood staring at the big tree for a long time. There was no sign of Ben.

His head was spinning. If Ben is *the* Ben, I've just spent four days learning math from a ghost. That isn't possible...is it? And if it is, how can a ghost play with a game? And he isn't around, anyway. I'd be stupid to leave my Game Boy here. Somebody'll steal it and I'll never see it again.

He spun around and walked quickly toward the gate. You're not real, Ben. You can't be, he said to himself as he began to jog toward home.

His parents took him out for pizza that night. To celebrate the great math mark, they said. When they got back home, Steve said he was tired and went to his room. He lay on his bed, trying to make sense of what had happened.

No matter how hard he tried, though, the one thing he couldn't forget was the smile on Ben's face when he'd agreed to let him have the Game Boy for a night. And his own words kept coming back to him. A deal's a deal, he'd said.

Steve looked at his watch. It was still only eight-thirty. He got up, grabbed his Game Boy and headed downstairs.

"I forgot something in the schoolyard," he shouted as he ran out the door. "I'll be right back."

It was nearly dark when he got to the school. He walked slowly across the empty baseball diamond to the tree. No one was there. It's too late, he thought. Ben got tired of waiting. Maybe he even saw me leave after school.

"Ben, I'm sorry," he whispered.

Then, he saw it — the hole in the trunk where kids sometimes hid secret messages. He reached up and felt inside. It was a small space, but big enough. He looked around to make sure no one was watching. Then he set his Game Boy carefully in the hole.

"Here it is, Ben. Have fun," he whispered and walked away.

When he got home, he crawled into bed and fell asleep wondering if he'd ever see his Game Boy again.

The next morning, Steve got to school early. Again, he looked around to make sure he was alone. Then he reached into the hole.

The Game Boy was there, exactly where he'd left it. No one has touched it, he thought. I was too late, after all. Well, at least I've got it back. Somehow, though, this thought didn't make him happy.

When he pulled out the Game Boy, he was surprised to find the power turned on. I must have pushed the On button when I grabbed it, he thought. Then he looked at the screen. Under the Game Over message was an incredibly high score.

Steve hit Start. The familiar *Tetris* tune began and there, on the opening screen, were three high scores. The one he'd already seen was listed first, with two others close behind.

Someone had used the game — someone who was a fast learner and a good teacher, too.

"I hope you had fun, Ben," Steve whispered. "It's easy once you get the hang of it, isn't it?" Just like math, he added silently.

He shut off the power and stuffed the Game Boy into his bag. As he walked toward the school, he glanced back at the tree. There was nobody there but, just in case, he waved.

A Dream
Come True

Jennifer's voice cut through the silence in the kitchen. "I found it. It's real," she called out happily. Startled, Morgan Ross spilled the coffee he was pouring. He hadn't realized she was back.

"What's real, dear?" he asked, grabbing a paper towel to wipe up the puddle.

"The house, Dad. The one in my dream. I found it all by myself," Jennifer beamed with pride.

"Right — how could I forget?" Morgan muttered under his breath as he dumped the soggy paper towel into the garbage. For the past nine months, he and his wife had listened to Jennifer's endless detailed descriptions of the house in her dream. The big white house with a porch and an attic. The only house where she could stay, where she could be happy again.

For nearly as long, he and Helen had tried to find that house, week after week, house after house. At first, it had been exciting, but now the whole business was starting to get to him. They'd looked at more than thirty houses, but none had been the right one for Jennifer.

He was beginning to wonder if the house existed at all. Still, it was wonderful to have his daughter around, talking and looking happy again. So, he smiled as he turned back to her, trying to look interested.

"Where is it?" he asked. This time? he added silently.

"Well, it's a little far from here," Jennifer began, "out by Millbrook." Then her excitement took over. "But, Dad, it's amazing. It's got a huge attic, and a porch and library and apple trees and everything. Just like I dreamed."

Dreamed! Morgan thought, briefly tuning out his daughter again. Not dreamed, as in once or twice, but dreamed as in many dreams, night after night. Ever since the accident. And always the same dream, she says. About that house. A big house. White, with shutters. The friendly house, she calls it. But what if there is no friendly house? What if there is no dream? What if...?

"So, will you call her now? Dad, are you listening?" Jennifer asked impatiently.

"Yes, dear, of course. Helen, could you come in here, please? Jennifer wants you," Morgan called out.

"Not Mom, Mrs. Jackson!" She rolled her eyes in frustration.

Mrs. Jackson was the real estate agent. She'd been showing them houses ever since they'd decided to move. But lately, Morgan thought, she seemed to be getting a little fed up with them.

Just last week she had said, "I've shown you every single big white house within a hundred kilometres, Mr. Ross. I don't know where to look next. Maybe you should take a break from house hunting for a while. Your wife seems very tired these days. Besides, you've got a lovely home already."

At that point, Morgan had stopped her.

"Not a home, Mrs. Jackson. Just a house. We must move. But, it has to be a house that's right for Jennifer."

"You said she's only eleven, Mr. Ross. I'm sure she'd get used to any house you bought." Impatience was creeping into Mrs. Jackson's voice.

"She's our only child, Mrs. Jackson." Morgan sighed. "You know how it is. We want her to be happy. That's all that ever mattered to us. So, if you'll just keep looking…"

And that's how they'd left it, with Mrs. Jackson promising to call as soon as she found something. But she hadn't sounded keen.

"What is it, Morgan?" Helen Ross asked, coming

quietly into the kitchen.

It was true. She was looking worn out lately. And pale too. No sparkle left. No get-up-and-go. But when she saw Jennifer, she perked up a little.

"Oh, you're back, dear. Are you all right? You look…" she frowned thoughtfully, "different somehow."

"I'm so happy, Mom. And guess why? I found the friendly house at last. It's perfect."

"Do you really think so, Jennifer?"

"I know so. I went there three times. They're there, Mom. Like in the dream. I saw them."

"Jennifer wants us to call Mrs. Jackson, Helen," Morgan interrupted. "To see if the house is for sale. But I'm not so sure…"

"Do it, dear. We can't stay here. You know that. It's the only way."

"All right. I'll call from the den," Morgan said. "Tell me again, Jennifer, exactly where this place is so I can pin it down for Mrs. Jackson."

Five minutes later, he was back in the kitchen, and he was smiling.

"She says it's listed."

Jennifer let out a whoop.

"It's been on the market for more than four years," Morgan continued. "But she says it's in such bad shape that she never dreamed of showing it to us."

"Don't worry, Dad. It's perfect. You'll see." Jennifer was so excited that she was flitting around the kitchen.

"Should you start packing? When do we move? Let's go."

"Calm down, Jennifer," Morgan said. "You know you have to save your energy. We'll go and see the house tomorrow."

"Tomorrow?" Helen asked.

"Mrs. Jackson is busy today," Morgan explained. "She'll get the key tomorrow and meet us there in the evening. Around eight."

Millbrook was only a half-hour drive from Fenton, but Jennifer was so eager to show off the house that the Rosses had agreed to leave at six.

"So you can see it when it's still bright out," Jennifer had explained. "I'll show you the way when you get close."

"We could bring along some food and have a picnic first," Morgan had suggested hopefully. It had been a long time since Helen had wanted to do anything like that, and he wasn't sure what she'd say. But she had agreed, saying that it sounded like a great idea — until he'd mentioned the lake.

"We could spread out a blanket by the lake, like we used to, and…"

That's when Helen had gone pale again.

"Not the lake, Morgan," she had whispered hoarsely. "You know I can't go back there. Not since Jennifer..." Her voice trailed off into silence.

"No, of course not," Morgan had said quickly, reaching out to take his wife's hand. "I wasn't thinking."

Instead, he had proposed stopping along the way for hot dogs and ice cream, and Helen had said she'd like that a lot.

And that's exactly what they'd done. But it was still only seven-thirty when they turned off Highway 52 onto County Road 10.

Almost immediately, Jennifer spoke up from the back seat. "Keep a lookout, Dad. We're nearly there. See that gate up ahead on the left? Turn in there."

Morgan wheeled the car slowly down a long, tree-shaded lane.

"There it is. Isn't it beautiful?" Jennifer said softly, as the car pulled into a clearing.

"Well, it's certainly big enough," said her dad, shutting off the ignition.

"And it was white once," added her mother dubiously, as they got out of the car.

Jennifer skipped ahead of her parents.

"Come on, you two. Hurry up. Wait till you see

inside," she called from the huge porch that ran around three sides of the house. Tall, shuttered windows opened onto it from each side of the front door.

"We have to wait for Mrs. Jackson," her dad called back. "She has the key."

"Oh, that's right. I forgot. You two need a key to get in," Jennifer giggled. Then she began to call out, "I'm here. I'm here," and drifted around the side of the house.

"All the patio furniture would fit on this porch," Morgan said, leading his wife up the steps after a walk around the property. "What do you think, Helen?"

"What do I think? I think that Jennifer will be happy here. Listen to her, Morgan. And did you see her when she got out of the car? She was positively glowing."

At that moment, Mrs. Jackson pulled into the lane and parked.

"Sorry I'm late," she called out as she grabbed her briefcase and hurried toward the porch.

"We're early," Morgan said. "And watch the steps. They need a little work."

"A little work? A lot of work, Mr. Ross. This whole place needs lots and lots of work. No one has lived here for years." Mrs. Jackson jumped back suddenly. "What's that? Did you hear that?"

"What?" Helen asked. "I didn't hear anything."

"Oh, I guess it's just me," Mrs. Jackson said. "Are you sure you want to see this place? It gives me the jitters. I can't imagine an eleven-year-old liking it. Did you finally bring Jennifer with you this time? I'd like to meet her."

I was right, Morgan thought. She *is* fed up with us.

Aloud, he simply said, "I told you she's uncomfortable with strangers. Now, can we go in and look around, please?"

Reluctantly, Mrs. Jackson pulled out a key, opened the door, and led the Rosses into the entrance hall.

Fifteen minutes later, she was edging back toward the hall, waiting impatiently for the Rosses to come downstairs.

Helen emerged from a bedroom and waved to her from the upstairs landing.

"I just wanted to take another look at the master bedroom," she said. "We're ready now."

Morgan joined her at the top of the stairs and, together, they slowly descended. They were smiling.

"We'll take it, Mrs. Jackson. When can we move in?" Morgan said.

Mrs. Jackson's cheeks turned bright red. "But you haven't even asked the price yet. Mind you, that won't be a problem. It's very low — less than half what your own house is worth. But..." she hesitated.

"But what?" Helen asked.

"Look, Mrs. Ross. I'd be lying if I said I didn't want this sale. I've spent more time with you people than I have with any other clients. I mean, we've been looking for nearly nine months. But I really don't think you should buy this house. And not just because of the state it's in."

"Why not?" asked Morgan.

Mrs. Jackson hesitated again, then continued. "This afternoon, when I stopped to pick up the key from the local real estate agent, he…" she paused.

"Go on," Helen said.

"Well, he told me something about the house." Mrs. Jackson lowered her voice. "Of course, I don't believe stuff like this myself, but he said some people think it's haunted."

"Really?" Helen said. "Tell us more."

Mrs. Jackson looked around nervously. Speaking nearly in a whisper, she continued, "Well, apparently a family used to live here, the Moranos. They had two children — a girl eleven and a boy thirteen. Five years ago, there was a terrible crash on Highway 52. Their car went off the bridge. Mr. and Mrs. Morano were saved, but not the children. They drowned. The Moranos left the house about a month later. The children had loved it out here in the country, but the house was too empty without them. It held too many memories for the parents. They just had to move."

Helen's eyes grew misty. "I know just how they felt." Then she added, "How sad. It's always terrible to lose a child."

"But," Mrs. Jackson said, speaking quickly now, "people say the children aren't really lost, gone, whatever. Some say they're still here. They say they've seen them. The two of them. Playing out in the yard, and moving past the windows late at night. Some people say they've even heard them singing. Laughing too. And just last week, the agent says he saw *three* shapes at the window, not just two. Even he is starting to believe the stories."

Mrs. Jackson's cheeks were burning now. "So do you see why you probably shouldn't buy this house? Besides, your daughter will hate it. She'll be scared to death of the place."

Mrs. Jackson was opening the door now, ushering the Rosses onto the porch. Then she froze. "Did you hear that?" she croaked.

"Hear what?" Morgan asked, stepping outside.

"I thought I heard someone laughing."

"Where? Inside?" he asked.

"No, over there," Mrs. Jackson said, pointing toward a small, neglected orchard. "But there's nothing there."

Helen and Morgan looked toward the orchard. In the glow of the sunset, they could just make out the

misty shapes of three children, two girls and a boy. They were darting in and out among the old apple trees as if they were playing tag.

Helen and Morgan looked back at each other and smiled.

"We'll take the house, Mrs. Jackson," they said together.

"But your daughter... You said she didn't want all the other houses. I'm sure she'll hate this one."

"I don't think so," Morgan said. "I think she'll find it a very friendly house, don't you, Helen?"

"I know she will," Helen said. "She'll probably say it's a dream come true."

Voice from the Past

Alex was not happy. It was still light out — a warm evening in May and a Saturday, too — and he was stuck in his room. He punched his pillow in frustration. If he hadn't talked back to his mother at dinner, he wouldn't be in his bedroom. But he had, and she had imposed her usual sentence.

"To your room," she had ordered, "and no food, no friends, no phone calls. You obviously need time to calm down. Three hours should do it."

Three hours! She was the one who needed three hours. It had only taken him about ten minutes. He'd already forgotten what had made him so angry.

Alex flipped onto his back and stared at the ceiling. Nothing exciting there, not even a cobweb dangling. He turned to the walls. They were covered with his favourite Blue Jays posters. Vernon Wells and Orlando Hudson had signed theirs for him. Carlos Delgado, Roberto Alomar and Joe Carter were up there, too. Those were his dad's. He had been a Blue Jays fan ever since he was a kid, and loved telling Alex what it had been like in Toronto the night the Jays won their first World Series. "Nearly a million people out on Yonge Street celebrating," he'd say. "You would have loved it, Alex."

I would have loved seeing tonight's game, too, Alex thought. If his mother hadn't needed so much time to calm down, he'd be downstairs watching it on TV. Instead, he switched on his radio, hoping to catch a score.

They must be in the second inning by now, he thought, as he tried to tune in the game.

"The pitch was low and inside." The announcer's voice filled the room. "It's two and 0 for Wells. Anderson winds up…"

Suddenly the voice was gone, replaced by nerve-grating, crackling static.

Alex fiddled with the dial. Static everywhere. He switched to FM. More static, and it seemed to be getting louder, even though he'd turned down the volume. Tapping the radio and shifting it around made no difference. He got up and checked the plug and cord. Nothing wrong there.

Then he felt it — a blast of icy air. He turned to the window. It was open, but the sunset was picture-perfect and the leaves on the tree outside were per-

75

fectly still. Only the curtain was moving slightly, floating as if lifted by an invisible hand.

Alex began to shiver. He sat up and pulled the comforter around his shoulders, but it didn't help much. The room was getting colder by the minute, and the static was getting louder too. He slipped an arm outside the comforter and hit the radio's Off button.

The silence that followed was nearly as disturbing as the static. It was absolute. Then Alex noticed the fog. It was rolling in over the windowsill and collecting on the floor near his closet.

He jumped up and headed for the window, dragging his comforter behind him. Just as he was about to slam the window shut, he heard another noise. It was low at first, like a hoarse whisper.

Alex hesitated. The sound grew louder. As he began to pull down the window, the sound became a voice — an eerie, tortured voice that uttered an unearthly, "Nooooooooooo."

Alex pulled back his hand and listened. Nothing.

I'm losing it, he thought, reaching for the window again. Once more, he heard it.

"Nooooooooooooooooooo."

He began to shake, and not just because he was cold. The sound seemed to be coming from near the closet. Slowly, he made himself turn toward it.

The fog had become a cloud, a grey misty cloud rising from the floor. Alex watched, spellbound, as the cloud swirled higher and began to branch out. The branches began to thicken.

Horrified, he realized what was happening. The cloud was taking a human shape.

Alex opened his mouth to yell, but no sound came out. He tried to make a dash for the door, but his feet felt rooted to the floor. It was as if he were caught in his worst nightmare.

The last wisps of fog settled around the shoulders of the horrible apparition, transforming into long, scraggly hair.

Alex found himself staring into a pair of milky white eyes. The spectre was wearing a long, old-fashioned coat, thick woollen pants and brown, mud-spattered boots. A thin scarf was wrapped around its neck, but its head and hands were bare.

Slowly, it stretched out its right hand. The bony fingers beckoned to Alex and the purple-tinged lips struggled to mouth a sound.

"*Commmmmmme.*"

Alex tried to yell. He had to warn his family. They had to get out of there.

"Aaugh!" he finally managed to shriek. "Mom, help. Help! Upstairs. Hurry!"

He heard her racing up the stairs. The door swung

open and there she stood, looking very worried.

"What's wrong, Alex? Did you hurt yourself?"

"Be careful, Mom. Don't come any farther. Just look, look!" He pointed at the apparition. "What is it, Mom? Get me out of here. Please! I can't move."

His mother raised her eyebrows and placed her hands on her hips.

"Look at what, Alex? What am I supposed to see?" she asked sharply.

"That!" Alex yelled, waving his arm frantically. "There, by the closet."

His mother was angry now.

"What is this, Alex? Some kind of trick so you can get downstairs to watch the game?"

"Mom, please," Alex begged. "It's a ghost or something. Can't you see it? It's right beside you."

At this, the corners of the apparition's mouth turned up in a ghastly smile.

"Alex, this is not funny. One more stunt like this and you can forget about TV for the rest of the month. And close that window. It's cold in here."

With that, she spun around and stormed out of the room, walking straight through the spectre's grotesque, outstretched hand before slamming the door behind her.

Once more, the hand began to beckon.

"*Commmmmmme, you are miiiinnne,*" the thing

wheezed, taking a shaky step toward Alex.

Alex jerked backwards. Surprised that he could move again, he wasn't prepared for what followed. His foot caught in the tangled comforter, and he crashed to the floor.

As the spectre slowly drifted toward him, its arms outstretched and its face distorted in a hideous grin, he tried to untangle himself.

Suddenly, he heard his father shouting downstairs.

"Ghost? He said a ghost?"

"But, Carl, there was nothing there."

Alex heard his father's footsteps on the stairs. He was taking the steps two at a time. From the sound of it, his mother was close behind.

"Dad. Mom. Help me," he called weakly.

His dad threw open the door. He stood, his face ashen, taking in the scene. His mom, looking bewildered, was right behind him.

"Are you all right, Alex?"

"Yes," Alex croaked.

Then his father looked directly at the apparition.

"Never!" he bellowed. "You can't have him."

Grim-faced, he pushed his startled wife to the safety of the hall. Then he turned to face the phantom.

As the sickly thing staggered closer to Alex, his father scanned the room. Suddenly, he spotted something.

"Alex, I want you to do exactly as I tell you."

Petrified, Alex could only nod.

"Reach out slowly and get the bat."

His dad was pointing to the Louisville Slugger leaning against the wall in the corner. It had been his. Carter, Alomar and Delgado had signed it for him back in 1992.

"Now, shove it over here. Quickly," he said.

Alex did as he was told. The creature stopped. It looked confused.

Alex's father snatched up the bat and looked frantically around the room.

"Please let this work," he muttered aloud. He grabbed a red marker from Alex's desk and scratched something on the bat. Then he gripped it with both hands and lunged straight at the ghoul. He swung wildly in all directions.

It was over in seconds. The apparition clawed the air and staggered backwards. It let out a blood-curdling scream and began to fade.

Alex's dad didn't stop swinging until the last icy wisp had disappeared. Then he dropped the bat and knelt beside Alex.

"He's gone. He's gone," he murmured, giving Alex a hug. "You're safe."

Mom edged into the room and joined in the hugging. Between sobs, she asked, "I couldn't see any-

thing, Carl. What was it? What was going on?"

"I'm not sure," Dad said, "but I'll tell you what I think."

The tale he told was strange, full of anger and feuding and a tragic death more than a hundred years ago in Eastern Europe.

"Apparently, my great-great-grandfather wanted the fighting to end. As a sign of good faith, he forbade his sons to carry weapons. But old hatreds don't die easily.

"One day, two of the sons were delivering some tables and chairs to the country house of a rich merchant. Back then, my family was known for making very fine furniture. On the way through the forest, the sons were ambushed. Desperate to defend himself, one of the boys broke off a table leg and started swinging. One of the other men was killed."

"So it was self-defence, right, Dad?"

"Yes, it was. But the head of the other family wouldn't accept that. It was his grandson who had been killed. The old man cursed my family. He said he would haunt us forever, coming back every generation to claim one male child. Because the fight had been between men, only the men would see him and only males would be claimed. I never believed the story — until today. I always thought my grandfather made it up to scare me."

"But, Dad, how did you know what to do?" Alex was still shaking.

"Well, I never believed my grandfather, but I did listen to every word. I remember him saying that the table leg the young man had used bore the family's mark."

He paused and pointed at the bat.

"The mark was a red star. I didn't know it would work, but I took a chance. What else could I do?"

Alex stared at the large red star scrawled on the bat. Then he noticed something.

"Oh no, Dad. Look what you did."

He pointed to the signature partially blotted out by the star. "You wrecked Joe Carter's autograph. He was your favourite."

"Don't worry, Alex. Carter was the greatest Blue Jay back in '93, but you're the greatest son ever. Carter wouldn't mind. He'd say it was worth it."

"Thanks, Dad," Alex said.

"So how about going downstairs and catching the end of the game?"

"That'd be great," Alex answered quickly, heaving a sigh of relief. "But," he added, turning to his mother, "my time isn't up yet, is it?"

"No," she said. "But I'd feel a lot better if we all stuck together right now. Let's go."

"Thanks, Mom, you read my mind."

Robber's Reward

The day started like any other. Julie's mother, a lab technician, left for the hospital around seven-thirty. Her dad wasn't home yet from another night of driving his cab. Julie and her sister fought over the bathroom and, as usual, she lost.

Finally, Ruby headed off to school — her classes started at eight-thirty — and Julie had a few minutes to herself. She flicked on the TV and began to crunch her way through a bowl of corn flakes.

The news was on — not exactly prime time viewing. Her thoughts wandered to the science fair topic she'd decided on last night. For once, she'd picked something she was really interested in.

She wanted to know why the shower curtain moved in and wrapped itself around her when she turned on the water. So did Ruby. She always screamed "Soap scum attack!" when it happened to her.

Her mom said a lot of science could be learned by

answering this question, and she was pretty smart about math and science. She wasn't so sure about her teacher, though. And he was the one who needed to give the green light to her topic this morning.

"...and police are still at the scene of the bank break-in at Fifth and Fraser..."

Fifth and Fraser! That was just three blocks away. Julie passed that corner every morning on the way to school. She suddenly tuned in to the newscaster's words.

"Reports are still sketchy, but it looks as if the alarm may have interrupted a burglary in progress. The first officers on the scene found a man, believed to be one of the suspects, dead in front of the vault. Detective Coleman of 22 Division refused to speculate about how the man died. He would say only that it's clear the dead man had not been alone in the bank. Police are asking people to avoid that intersection until..."

Julie jumped up from the table. She switched off the TV, dumped her bowl in the sink and tore into her bedroom. She grabbed her backpack, stopped off at the bathroom to give her teeth a two-second brush, and dashed out of the apartment.

A large crowd was gathered in front of the bank when Julie got there. She jostled her way through the people until she was stopped by a thick, yellow plastic ribbon that warned: Police Line — Do Not Cross.

Julie was fascinated. An ambulance, its red lights flashing, was parked near the door of the bank. Police cars and equipment vans emblazoned with the logos of the city's TV stations were everywhere. Reporters and camera crews were scurrying about, and police officers were questioning people on the street and controlling the parade of individuals moving into and out of the bank.

Through the bank's double entrance doors, Julie could just make out a small circle of people hovering over something on the floor. That must be where the body is, she thought. They never move it until they've looked for all the evidence. She knew that. It always happened that way on TV.

Suddenly, police officers moved to the doors and held them open as two uniformed paramedics began to walk slowly forward. Julie realized what was happening. They were bringing out the body.

The crowd grew silent as the paramedics emerged and loaded the stretcher carefully into the ambulance. Julie stared. It was exciting, but it bothered her, too. Someone had died. Somebody's brother, husband or even father.

"Husband *and* father," she heard a voice say.

"Huh?" Julie swung around to see who'd spoken. No one was paying any attention to her. She turned back, feeling foolish. For a second, she could have sworn someone had read her mind.

"I did. Weird, isn't it?" she heard the voice again.

Julie spun around. Again, no one was even looking her way. The crowd was thinning now. The person closest to her — an older woman — was several steps away. But the voice, a low, throaty whisper, had sounded as if it were right at her ear. It was a man's voice.

"I'm right here, kid."

Julie shivered. This is spooky, she thought. She'd heard voices before, at summer camp. But that had been Rachel McKenzie up to her usual tricks. She loved to wait until someone was asleep, then whisper weird noises in her ear. Rachel wasn't anywhere around. In fact, right now, Rachel was probably at school, waiting for the bell to ring.

And that's where I should be, too, Julie decided. Her mother always said her imagination worked overtime. Too much television, she'd say. It does things to your brain. Julie backed away from the yellow tape and started to jog along Fifth Street toward the school.

"Slow down, kid. I'm new at this."

The voice was following her. She was sure of it now. Terrified, Julie began to run.

"Wait. This is using up too much energy."

Julie felt a tugging at her back. She stopped and whipped around. Nothing. There was nothing there. She was petrified, too scared to move. She stood rooted to the spot, her knees knocking and her stomach churning.

"Sorry, kid. But it worked. You stopped. Now will you listen to me, please?"

Julie detected a note of desperation in the voice. Stay or go? School was just two blocks away. Go to school. You'll be safe there, she thought.

"Maybe not. I haven't gone through any walls yet, but I'm willing to try. Besides, there's always a window."

"All right, all right," Julie muttered, trying not to move her lips. She looked around to see if anyone had heard. She didn't want any of the other kids to see her talking to herself. Luckily, the coast was clear, for the moment.

She ducked up an alley and stammered, "Who... whoever or...whatever you are...what do you want from me?"

I can't believe I'm doing this, she thought. I'm talking to it, whatever *it* is. Am I crazy or what?

"You're not crazy. But I was...and now I'm dead. And I shouldn't be, you know."

Suddenly, the metal lid from a battered garbage can clattered to the pavement next to her. Julie jumped as the sound echoed up and down the alley. Then she heard rustling in the can. She stood perfectly still. More rustling, and some scratching. Julie stopped breathing. More scratching. Her imagination shifted into high gear. What sort of spectre was about to materialize?

When a scraggly tabby cat poked its face over the top of the can and blinked at her, Julie let out a long, slow sigh of relief. The cat jumped lightly to the ground and ran off. Julie was tempted to follow. Instead, she looked around one more time to make sure she was alone.

Alone? That's funny, she thought. I wish I really were alone. Then it hit her. Whatever it was, it had figured out what she was thinking. She hated the idea of someone being in her head like that. But it would take care of the problem of getting caught talking out loud to empty space.

What are you? Julie thought. What do you want from me?

Silence. She concentrated harder. What do you want? Not a sound. It's gone! Or I'm sane again, she thought. This might be her chance to escape. She turned to leave.

"Stop, please. Don't go." The voice was coming from her right, over by the wall.

Julie's fear returned. She shut her eyes and concentrated even harder. What do you want?

"Please, say something. Say you'll help."

"Why do I have to say something?" Julie whispered. "You know what I'm thinking."

"I can't seem to do that anymore. It started when they loaded me onto the stretcher. I knew what the cops were thinking. Then, when they wheeled me out to the ambulance, all sorts of thoughts came flooding in. All those people. It was rough. That crowd was pretty hostile. Some ugly thoughts out there. Except for you. You thought about my family."

The voice paused briefly. Julie thought she heard a sob. Then the voice went on.

"That's why I picked you. But I can't read your mind anymore. In fact, I don't know how much time I have left. Everything is starting to feel different. Will you help me?"

The impact of what she'd just heard hit Julie in the stomach like a baseball bat.

"You're the…" Julie gulped. "You're the…uh… man at the bank?"

"The dead guy. Yeah."

Julie gasped. "Ok-k-kay," she sputtered, trying to sound calm. "I have to go now. I'm going to get it. I'm really late for school."

"Don't go. Not yet. I have to set the record straight. You've got to help me do that. Please, for my boy's sake," the voice pleaded.

"But why should I help you? You're a..."

"A thief? A crook? Say it, kid. It's true. I know it was really stupid, but I needed the money and... well... I let my friend talk me into it. But it was the first time. Really. You've got to believe me."

"I don't know what to believe anymore."

"I know how you feel. But listen, please. First, my name's Jim. Jim Robertson. And you're...?"

"Julie." Julie hesitated. Last names made it easier for someone to find you. Then she realized how ridiculous that thought was. This thing, this spirit, this ghost could probably find her anywhere, any-time.

"Sharma," she added. "Julie Sharma." There. I've done it. I just introduced myself to a ghost.

"Pleased to meet you, Julie. I'm telling the truth. It really was the first time. It's no excuse, I know, but things were bad. I'd lost my job. My wife and son had left, the rent was overdue and the landlord was threatening to throw me out of the apartment.

"So Nick — my best friend, Nick — came up with this plan. Nothing to it, the lying scumbag said. He used to work at the bank as a security guard. I know the layout, he said. No one'll get hurt. Ha. What a joke!"

"What went wrong?" Julie was surprised to find herself interested.

"Nothing, at first. Everything went like clockwork until…"

Suddenly, everything became clear to Julie. "Until he tricked you," she blurted. "When he didn't need you anymore, he killed you, right, and took the money for himself?"

"That's right. And now Nick'll get away with the money — and with murder. My murder. And the truth will never come out. Not that it's so pretty. But, if the cops get Nick, maybe my ex-wife will understand a little better. Maybe she'll be able to explain things to the boy when he's bigger. I'm not all bad, you know." The voice trailed off at that point.

Julie had a minute to think. I'm already in big trouble. School started half an hour ago. And not even the most gullible teacher will believe this story. Aloud she said, "Okay, what can I do?"

"Thanks, kid," the voice sounded relieved, but tired. It seemed to be growing fainter. "Here's what you can do. There's this crime tip number…"

"I know. I hear it on TV all the time. It's 577-…"

"Good, you know it. We'll go to that pay phone over there. If you dial the number for me, I'll tell them what happened at the bank. They won't know it's me. They'll just think I'm a sleazeball turning in a friend. And they'll be right, won't they? I'll give them my good old friend, Nick."

"That's it? That's all you want?"

"That's it. If I could do it myself, I would."

"Okay, let's go then," Julie said, reaching into her pocket for a quarter.

Julie dialed the number and kept the receiver to her ear as a deep voice answered, "Constable Tremblay. Thank you for calling Crime Tips."

Julie could almost feel Jim leaning beside her. Shivers rippled down her spine.

"Hello," Jim said, "I know what happened at…"

"Hello?" Tremblay repeated. "Is anybody there?"

Julie held out the phone a little farther, trying to figure out how to make it easier for Jim to speak into the receiver.

"I'm here," Jim spoke up. "A man named Nick…"

"Is anyone there? Hello?" Tremblay said loudly.

"He can't hear me, kid! He can't hear me," Jim said, panic in his voice. "What'll I do? Can you hear me? Am I gone?"

"I hear you," Julie said, covering the mouthpiece. "But maybe I'm the only one who can."

"Oh no," Jim moaned.

Julie looked at the receiver in her hand. She swallowed hard and put the phone back to her ear.

"I'm sorry," she began nervously. "I dropped the phone."

Shakily, she told the officer what she'd learned.

Jim helped, whispering the answers to the officer's questions. Julie even managed to work in information about where Nick planned to hide the money — in a locker at the bus terminal.

She could almost feel Jim nodding enthusiastically when she added that if the police staked out the terminal, they could probably catch Nick red-handed when he went to pick up the money.

But when Tremblay asked how to get the reward to her if the tip led to an arrest, Julie panicked. She covered the mouthpiece.

"Go for it," Jim whispered hoarsely. "You earned it. You don't have to give your name. They'll work out something with you."

Julie was tempted. Crime Tips paid $1,000 if an arrest was made. But somehow it didn't seem right to take it, and she wasn't sure why.

"Just a minute, please," she said, and covered the mouthpiece again.

"Jim, what's your wife's name?"

"Maria," Jim answered faintly. "Maria Lopez. She went back to her own name."

"And her address?"

"1394 Merton, Apartment 1B. Why?"

Julie spoke quickly into the phone, "The reward goes to Maria Lopez, 1394 Merton, Apartment 1B. Goodbye." She hung up and slumped against the wall

of the phone booth. Her knees were trembling.

Weakly, Jim said, "Thanks, Julie. You're something else. Your folks must be really proud of you."

At the mention of her folks, Julie panicked and pushed her way out of the phone booth.

"Well, they won't be if the school called already to find out why I'm not there. I've really gotta go."

"So do I, kid. I think my time's nearly up."

"Well...good luck."

What an unbelievably dumb thing to say! Julie thought. Then she started to run. There'd be time to think later, after she got to school.

By the time she reached her homeroom, Julie had decided to go with a version of the truth. As Mr. Falconi glared at her, she explained that she'd stopped to watch what was going on at the bank and lost track of time.

Mr. Falconi lectured her on the evils of lateness, then levelled a parting shot. "And I suppose you also lost track of your science fair topic."

"No, I've got that."

"Well, what is it? How to investigate bank robberies in three easy lessons?" Some of the kids giggled.

"No...it's to find out why the curtain moves in toward you when you turn on the shower." That started even more giggles.

"What did you say? You're on thin ice already, Ms. Sharma. This is no time for joking."

"I'm not joking, Mr. Falconi."

Julie heard a faint whisper in her ear. "The window, kid. Look. Hurry."

Oh no, Julie thought. I can't take this.

"Hurry, kid. I haven't got much more time."

Julie looked at the open windows that lined the wall of the classroom. Shapeless blue drapes hung limply over them. Suddenly, a single pair of drapes swayed slightly, then pressed against the open window, as if they were being sucked outside.

"There, like that," Julie pointed at the window.

"Yeah, why does that happen?" Rachel McKenzie yelled.

"I guess Julie will find out and tell us," Mr. Falconi said. "I wonder why it happened at only one window."

"Probably just a fluke breeze," Julie offered, watching the drapes fall back into place. Once again, like the air outside, they were perfectly still. Thanks, Jim, she thought. Goodbye.

A Boy's Best Friend

Only one thing got Marshall through the miserable weeks after his dog, Fred, was hit by a car and killed. That was thoughts of summer camp.

Whenever memories of Fred started to get to him, he'd check the calendar over his desk and count off the days till camp was due to start.

Finally, it was the night before he was to leave for another magical summer at White Pine. Marshall picked up the picture of himself and Fred that he kept on his bedside table.

"G'night, buddy," he said, as he did every night. Then he tucked it into the side pocket of his bag, right next to his three new Gordon Korman books.

"White Pine, here I come," he thought as he snuggled under the covers. For the first time in months, he felt really and truly happy.

But his happiness was short-lived. It lasted through the two-hour bus ride to the camp and through the silly greetings the counsellors invented for the campers. But it ended abruptly the moment Marshall opened the door of his cabin.

There, on bed number six — right beside his — sat Zack Vincent, perpetrator of countless Zack Attacks. That's what the other campers called the things Zack did to his victims. Most of them had suffered through at least one Zack Attack.

Zack worked hard at keeping his reputation as the camp bully. Somehow, he must have sensed that Marshall was ripe for the picking. He launched his first attack right away.

"Well, well, well, if it isn't Sheriff. Or is it Deputy? No, wait. Now I've got it. It's Marrrrr-shull."

The way Zack said it, Marshall almost wished his name were Dumbo. He walked slowly over to his bed, trying to ignore the fact that the other boys were watching, waiting to see what he'd do. Tyler, a friend from last year, was the only one who might stick up for him.

"Hey, Marrrrr-shull. Where's your badge? You going to arrest me, Marrrrr-shull?"

Somebody should, Marshall thought, but he said nothing. He simply went about unpacking his bag, wishing with all his heart that his mother's expression, "Ignore it — it'll go away" were true.

But Zack wasn't going anywhere, and he was

impossible to ignore. In the next few days, he hid Marshall's runners, short-sheeted his bed, flipped a garter snake over the top of the stall while Marshall showered, and poured water into his bed while he slept.

Marshall woke embarrassed, convinced he'd wet his bed. It was only later, when he overheard Zack bragging about it, that he realized what had happened. He was living a nightmare and there was no end in sight.

That night after dinner, Marshall asked to be excused from campfire. It was the first time he'd done it, so the counsellors gave him permission.

Thankful for some time to himself, Marshall got ready for bed and scrunched down under the covers with his flashlight, a book and his picture of Fred. He'd been using it as a bookmark all through camp. That way he could sneak a peek at it as often as he wanted.

Tyler had asked about Fred. Tyler had a dog, too — Bowser. The previous summer, he and Marshall had spent a lot of time swapping dog stories.

This summer, though, there was no more dog talk. Tyler didn't want to hurt Marshall's feelings by going on about how great Bowser was. And Marshall didn't dare talk about Fred for fear he'd start to cry. Zack would have a field day if he ever caught Marshall bawling like a baby.

Fred and Zack. The two had become woven together in Marshall's mind. The more Zack tormented him, the more he longed to have Fred back.

He stared at Fred's picture, wishing he could make him materialize. Then it wouldn't matter what Zack did to him.

Fred and Zack. Zack and Fred. Marshall forced his eyes to stay open just long enough so he could switch off his flashlight and stuff his book — and bookmark — under his pillow. Then he curled up on his side, his back to Zack's bed, and fell asleep.

It was still dark when Marshall woke up, covered in sweat and shaking like Jell-O. The nightmare again. The one that had haunted him ever since camp started.

In it, Marshall stood over Zack, watching him choke on a peanut butter sandwich. Fred was there too, yapping and biting at Zack's ankles. As Zack writhed helplessly on the cabin floor, Marshall felt himself starting to laugh — a loud, gloating cackle that turned his blood to ice. As Zack gasped and held out his hands for help, Marshall turned his back and walked toward the door.

But the door was covered by an enormous piece of paper. On it, scrawled in huge letters, was a Chinese proverb: *He who seeks revenge should dig two graves.* Marshall had seen it before — in English class when his teacher used it to introduce a story about a man trying to get even with a friend who had betrayed him.

The paper swayed, blocking Marshall's exit. Still laughing horribly, he tore through it and pushed his way outside.

For a moment, he felt himself floating. In the dark below were two freshly dug graves. Zack's lifeless body lay in one. Then he started to fall.

That's when he always woke up. Every night. Right on cue. His arms flailing, struggling to stop himself from falling into the second grave.

The cabin was quiet, except for the rhythmic buzz of Tyler's snoring. As his eyes adjusted to the darkness, Marshall could just make out Zack, lying on his side, facing him. Zack was sound asleep, a smile creasing the corners of his mouth.

He's probably dreaming about what he's going to do to me tomorrow, Marshall thought. I wish he'd disappear. And, most of all, I wish you were here, Fred. I'd sic you on that creep. You'd teach him a thing or two. Geez, I miss you, little buddy.

Marshall eventually fell asleep again, his eyes moist with secret, silent tears.

Things got worse the next morning. His tossing and turning during the night must have knocked his book to the floor. He woke up to find Zack waving Fred's picture in front of his eyes.

"So, who's this, Marrrrr-shull? Your girlfriend? Hey, guys, Marshall's girlfriend is a real dog." Zack laughed mockingly. Some of the other kids joined in weakly.

"Give it back," Marshall said, trying to get up. Zack leaned over and shoved the picture into Marshall's face.

"Give it back," Marshall mumbled.

Zack didn't budge. Suddenly Marshall pulled back both legs and kicked with all his might. Zack tumbled to the floor. Marshall followed, in a tangle of sheets and blankets.

"Give it to me, Zack. Right now. It's mine." Zack scrambled to his feet and moved to the other side of the bunk.

"Marshall's girlfriend's a dog. Marshall's girlfriend's a dog," he taunted.

Marshall struggled to stand up. As he got to his feet, he tripped on the sheet and fell across Zack's bed. Desperately, he grabbed for the picture.

"You want it?" Zack jeered. "Here, have it." He ripped the photo apart, crumpled the pieces, and tossed them at Marshall. Then he turned and headed for the door.

Marshall picked up the pieces and stood up. Fighting back tears, he yelled, "You'll be sorry for this, Zack. You wait. You're nothing but a bully.

That's all. A scummy, scuzzy, brainless bully!"

Someone gasped. Then there was dead silence in the cabin. Shocked, everyone was quiet, including Marshall.

Slowly, Zack swung around and glared at him. Then, as if deciding that he'd done enough damage, he turned and strolled out the door.

Marshall tried to salvage the photograph. He spread out the pieces on his bunk, hoping he'd be able to tape them back together. It was no use. Fred's face was torn right down the middle and white cracks showed where Zack had crumpled the pieces. The picture was ruined. Fred was gone, and now so was his photograph.

Thoughts of Fred and what Zack had done weighed heavily on Marshall as he trudged to the dining hall for breakfast. He didn't dare line up at the steam table for scrambled eggs and sausages. That was a favourite place for Zack to carry out a sneak attack on his victims.

Instead, he went directly to his cabin's table where there was a supply of toast, cereal and juice. Before he sat down beside Tyler, he checked his chair to make sure Zack hadn't painted it with jam.

As if reading his mind, Tyler said, "Don't worry. He's not here."

"Where is he?" Marshall asked.

"Gone to have a shower," Tyler said, breaking into a grin. "He never made it to breakfast. He tripped and fell into the worst mud puddle around. Even some of the counsellors laughed."

"You're kidding."

"Nope. It was great. You should have been there."

Marshall was there the next time Zack tripped, on the way to lunch. And he was there when Zack stumbled on the way to the dock, too. He had his bathing suit on and skinned his knees badly.

Then he collapsed on the way to the campfire, letting out an agonized yell as he tumbled to his battered knees again. This time, Marshall actually winced in sympathy.

That night, Zack went to bed without tormenting anyone, not even Marshall. Marshall fell asleep smiling. At last Zack was getting exactly what he deserved.

For the first time since camp started, Marshall slept peacefully and woke feeling refreshed. Zack, however, woke up grumpy as a grizzly bear, complaining that he'd nearly frozen to death.

"...and whoever kept pulling off the covers better watch out," he threatened. "When I catch him, he'll wish he'd never been born."

He glared straight at Marshall as he said this. Then he snatched his blankets off the floor and began to make his bed.

Marshall made his own bed quickly, anxious to get as far from Zack as possible. In a mood like that, there was no telling what he might do.

Mind you, Marshall thought, losing your blankets like that could be really irritating, especially on a cool night. He remembered how Fred sometimes used to pull off his covers. He hated waking up chilled to the bone.

That day, strange things continued to happen to Zack. In the morning, he fell backwards off the dock, claiming a horsefly had taken a huge chunk out of his ankle. But when the waterfront director offered him After-Byte to rub on the spot, Zack could find no sign of swelling or redness anywhere.

At dinner — a wiener roast around the fire — Zack claimed that someone snatched his hot dog. Even though he'd cooked it and drowned it in ketchup himself, he was convinced that someone had tied a string to it and yanked it away.

When the counsellors told him to lighten up, he flew into a rage and stormed off. He was lying in bed, his face pressed into his pillow, when the others returned.

The next morning, the cabin woke to more of Zack's ranting.

"If I catch that dog, I'll stuff him in a sack with a big rock and heave him into the lake."

"What dog?" Tyler asked.

"The one that yapped outside all night."

"I didn't hear any dog," Tyler said. "Did you guys?"

The others, Marshall included, shook their heads, mystified.

"What do you mean, you didn't hear it? Are you deaf? Yap, yap, yap — all night long. I'm going to set a wolf trap out there tonight."

Zack's talk of a yapping dog reminded Marshall of Fred. Fred used to do that sometimes — yap, yap, yap, until he got what he wanted. Wait a minute, Marshall thought. Fred used to pull the covers off my bed, too. And snatch food at barbecues. That was one of his favourite tricks.

Suddenly, there was a loud crash followed by a scream. Zack lay sprawled at the bottom of the cabin steps. He was crying.

Giggles rippled through the cabin. The mighty Attacker was blubbering like a baby.

Someone called out "Wacko Zacko" and the giggles turned to hoots of mocking laughter. Everyone was laughing. Everyone except Tyler, who never laughed at other people's troubles — and Marshall.

Marshall wasn't laughing because he'd just added another item to his mental list. Fred was always underfoot. It seemed like someone was forever tripping

over him. This is impossible, Marshall thought. It can't be. Fred is…

Zack screamed again. Tyler and Raj, who were trying to help him up, jumped back.

"My leg," Zack moaned, collapsing against Tyler. "I can't stand up. Get help. I think it's broken."

Marshall ran and collected two counsellors who used a firefighter's lift to carry Zack to the infirmary. Marshall and the others trailed behind, then hung around outside waiting for word on Zack's injury.

Finally, the nurse emerged to announce that Zack's leg wasn't broken, but it was badly sprained.

"He'll be spending the next couple of days in the infirmary," he said.

The rest of the day was great. With Zack safely out of commission, everyone relaxed. Everyone except Marshall. He struggled to come up with an explanation for what was happening. Every time, he got the same impossible answer — Fred.

Later that evening, when the other kids were changing into their bathing suits for a midnight swim, Marshall slipped off to the infirmary. Quietly, he skulked around it. Then, he stood statue-still under the window and listened intently. He saw and heard nothing unusual.

Finally, he crouched in the darkness and whispered, "Fred, Fred. Here boy. C'mere, boy." Nothing.

Nevertheless, he went on.

"Listen to me, boy. I think you're out there. If you are, thanks. You really came through. But, Fred, it's over now, okay? I can't stand to see Zack feeling like I did. Give the guy a break, Fred. He's got no friends. I'm okay now, fella. Really, I am."

As Marshall stood up to leave, he stepped on a stick. It snapped with a loud crack.

"Who's there?" Zack called out sharply. Fear filled his voice. "Is that you, dog?"

Marshall wavered. Should I answer — or just get out of here? He sounds really scared.

"It's me, Zack. Marshall."

"What are you doing out there?" Some of the bravado was returning to Zack's voice.

"Oh...I just came by to say good night."

"Yeah?" Zack sounded surprised.

"Yeah," Marshall said, pushing open the door. In the glow of a night light, Marshall could just see Zack's head poking out from under the covers.

"Shhh," Zack whispered. "The nurse might not be asleep yet. He just finished putting ice on my ankle a while ago."

"How's the leg?" Marshall whispered back.

"It hurts."

"Sorry."

"So am I."

Marshall couldn't believe his ears. "What did you say?" he asked.

"I said, 'So am I'." Zack looked like he was bracing for Marshall to say something mean.

Marshall stared. Then he said softly, "It's okay."

Zack let out his breath and his face softened. "Thanks," he said.

"No problem. See you in the morning?"

"Sure."

Marshall tiptoed back to his cabin and slipped into bed. By the time the others got back from their swim, he was sound asleep. He dreamed that Fred was curled up at the foot of his bed.

After breakfast, Marshall returned to the infirmary. Zack was sitting up, eating breakfast. "How's the leg?" Marshall asked.

"Much better, thanks."

"Great," said Marshall. "Does it still hurt?"

"Not too much. I think the nurse must have put a heating pad on it in the night. I remember waking up and thinking how good it felt to have something soft and warm tucked around my ankle."

Marshall looked at the foot of the bed, then at Zack. Smiling, he said, "Yeah, I know just what you mean."

Wall-to-Wall Horror

From the day we moved into the old house on Hill Street, I felt like someone was watching us. It was nothing I could pin down. Just a feeling that came over me every now and then, especially when I was alone.

Sometimes, it happened while I was watching TV in the living room. Suddenly, I'd think my older brother, Kyle, was trying to sneak up and scare me, a favourite trick of his. I'd whip around to catch him — only he wouldn't be there.

I never mentioned it to anybody. For sure, Mom and Dad would think I was going nuts — and I might have agreed. When I got the creepy-crawly feeling, I just tried to ignore it.

This got a lot harder, though, after Dad laid the new carpet in the den off the living room.

The den was a nice little room. Mom and Dad had furnished it with a rocking chair and an overstuffed couch they'd picked up at a garage sale. Dad built some shelves beside the small fireplace and Mom rewired an old lamp.

All in all, it was a cozy place, perfect for curling up with a good book. Except that I couldn't stay in the room for more than a few minutes. The feeling that someone was watching me was just too strong.

I wasn't the only one who was uncomfortable in there, either. It seemed like nobody ever stayed in the den for long. Mom blamed it on the carpet.

"I've tried three times to get rid of that disgusting stain right in the middle. It just won't come out," she said.

She got no argument from Dad. "A real amateur laid this carpet," he said. "It doesn't lie flat, it's buckling in the corners, and whoever did it never bothered to nail down the loose floorboards first. See where it's wearing out over those two ridges? Loose boards under there."

There wasn't much money to fix up the house — and it needed a lot of work. That's why they'd been able to afford it in the first place.

Fixing it up was going to take a long time, and we'd all have to pitch in. Well, Kyle and I would have to pitch in. Brian, who was four, and Sally, who was one and a half, were too young to do much but get in the way.

There was lots to do, but replacing the ugly carpet

in the den quickly moved to number one on the fix-it list.

Mom found a nice rose-coloured remnant that was nearly the right size and Dad trimmed and installed it in an afternoon. He'd been right about the loose floorboards. He nailed down four of them before laying the foam underpad.

When we moved the furniture back into the room, everyone agreed that it looked great. The first thing I did was bring down my library books to add to the collection on the shelves beside the fireplace. I could hardly wait to curl up on the couch with *Inkspell*. Surely now that the room looked so nice, it would feel nice, too.

How wrong I was. I lasted ten minutes. Then I couldn't stand it any longer. It felt as if every knot in the pine panelling was an eye, staring right at me.

The next afternoon, I tried again. No sooner had I settled down on the couch than the rocking chair started swaying gently back and forth — all by itself. I headed for the living room, trying to convince myself that it must have been the wind.

The next morning — Saturday — I slept late. I was still rubbing sleep out of my eyes when I started to wander downstairs around ten o'clock.

That's when I heard Mom yell, "Oh no!"

I flew down the last few steps and raced into the

living room. She was standing in the doorway to the den.

"Look," she said, pointing to the carpet.

"Geez," I said. The stain was back. Not as dark and not as big. But definitely there.

By this time, Dad and Kyle had arrived on the scene, too.

Mom asked Dad if he'd noticed anything wrong with the boards when he was nailing them down.

"Nope. They were just fine. Not oily or stained or anything. Just a little scratched and worn along the edges in some places, that's all. A few rough spots wouldn't do that," he said, pointing to the stain.

He looked puzzled. Then he turned to Kyle, with one of those "Ah-ha, I've got it" looks in his eyes.

"Okay, Kyle. Time's up. Not a bad trick. But it's time to confess. What is it, water? I'll have your head if you used something that will leave a mark."

"I didn't do anything, Dad," Kyle protested.

"It's not damp, Ron," Mom said. "I felt it."

"You, then?" Dad asked looking straight at me.

"Dad, this is not my style. Besides, thanks to my dear brother here, I know what it's like to be the butt of a joke like this."

As I spoke, I watched Kyle's face. He looked as baffled as I was. I was pretty sure he wasn't the culprit — but, if he wasn't, who was?

Mom decided that she wasn't going to spend the rest of the weekend scrubbing a rug.

"I'll rent a steam cleaner next week and do the bedrooms at the same time."

Even then, I had a feeling that steam cleaning wasn't likely to be the answer. And when I thought about it some more, I was sure.

By Sunday night, I knew I'd need Kyle's help. After dinner, I called him into the den. The rest of the family was in the living room watching TV.

"Look, can you see it?" I whispered, pointing to the rocking chair.

"That's weird. It's moving."

"Keep your voice down. But you can see it, too?" He nodded.

"That's a relief. I was beginning to think I was in big trouble up here." I tapped my head.

"Now look at this," I whispered, pointing to the stain on the carpet. "It's growing, Kyle. Take my word for it. And look here. The boards have lifted again."

"What is this, Lizzie — *The Twilight Zone* or something? We better tell Mom and Dad."

"No!" I said sharply, grabbing his arm. "I'm not finished. Listen, Kyle…" I swallowed hard. "Have you felt anything…odd…since we moved in here?"

He looked at me strangely.

"Like someone's watching you?" I added quickly.

"Come on, Kyle, the truth."

He took a deep breath, then let it out slowly. "A few times, yes. But there's nothing here, Lizzie. I've checked — lots."

"Why didn't you say anything?"

"And let you call me a wimp — or say that I was losing my marbles? Get serious!"

I grimaced. "I know exactly what you mean. I don't think Mom and Dad have noticed a thing. You know what they're like. They would have found a way to ask us without letting on that anything was wrong. I haven't picked up on anything like that, have you?"

He shook his head.

"Okay, so let's suppose they haven't noticed. Think about it, Kyle. If we say something, it'll take forever to get them to believe us."

"So, what do you suggest?" Kyle asked.

"Well, it's not as if anything really bad has happened. Whatever it is, I don't think it's trying to hurt us."

"I guess not." Kyle didn't sound totally convinced.

"So, I think it's trying to tell us something."

Kyle rolled his eyes and snorted, but I hurried on before he could interrupt.

"Just listen, okay? If we could figure out what it's trying to tell us, then maybe it would go away."

Suddenly, the rocking chair started moving again, more quickly this time. I grabbed Kyle's hand and held on tight.

"See, I'm telling you, Kyle," I said urgently. "It's giving us a sign that we're on the right track."

"I don't know, Liz." He still wasn't totally with me.

Before he could finish, though, my library books — no others, just mine — tumbled off the shelf, landing on the floor with a loud thump.

Kyle stared at the messy pile, then shrugged.

"All right. I believe, I believe. What do you want to do?"

The first thing I wanted to do was go upstairs. Now that my thoughts were actually in words, my skin was starting to crawl. I wanted out of that room.

Upstairs, I suggested that Kyle pump his new friend, Ian, for information about the people who had lived in the house before us.

"Ask him at school tomorrow, okay?"

The real estate agent had told us only that the owner had died of a heart attack and that a nephew in New York — his only relative — had arranged the sale through a lawyer. Ian had lived three houses away all his life, so he should know more than that.

"All right, I'll do it…but why?"

"Well," I began, trying to sound more confident than I felt, "because that's a good a place to start. In lots of the stories I've read, a ghost — if that's what this is — hangs around because it has unfinished business of some sort."

I'd read piles of ghost stories, so I knew what I was talking about. I'd even done an English project on a horror theme. But this was not a time for reading. This was a time for doing something about what might be a genuine horror story — with us as the main characters.

The next evening, at dinner, I had the strangest sensation. It felt as if something were hovering over us, like a cloud. But when I looked up at the ceiling, all I saw were a few cracks in the plaster. I was still staring at them when I realized Dad was talking to me.

"Earth to Lizzie."

"Oh, sorry. I wasn't paying attention."

"No kidding. I was just asking what you've been reading lately."

Dad was like that. He tried to ask each of us kids — even Sally — a question at dinner. He said it was to keep the fine art of conversation alive.

"Are you still on that horror kick, or have you moved on to other things?"

"I guess I'm sort of still on it, but not so much. Right now, I'm reading a really cool fantasy."

"Well, as long as you don't start believing in those ghosts and monsters…"

Dad never finished his sentence. Suddenly, he was on his feet, trying to shake off the hot coffee that had spilled across the table.

Mom, Kyle and I all jumped up at the same time, grabbing for the paper towels to wipe up the mess.

"Sorry about that," Dad said when things settled down. "I must have bumped it with my elbow."

I knew he hadn't, though. His elbow had been nowhere near his coffee mug. I sneaked another peek at the ceiling. Nothing there. My hand shook as I finished my milk.

After we did the dishes, Mom and Dad took Brian and Sally to Grandma's for a visit. I just hung around the house feeling nervous.

Finally, I heard Kyle come in from basketball practice. I was dying to hear what he'd found out from Ian. I raced down to the kitchen and sat at the table across from him while he wolfed down some warmed-over stew.

"So?" I said expectantly.

"You may be on to something," he said between mouthfuls. "I hate to think what, though."

"So, tell me. Tell me."

"Their name was Patterson. And it's true. Mr. Patterson died of a heart attack, like the agent said. But he'd been acting strange for a long time before that. Talking to himself, keeping all the lights on all night. Sometimes, he'd open the door and start yelling stuff like, 'Keep away. Leave me alone,' when no one was there. Everybody said he went crazy after his wife was declared dead."

"Declared dead? What do you mean?"

"Ian says she was reported missing about ten years ago. Just disappeared one day. He remembers hearing his mother tell someone that she probably left because Mr. Patterson was so grumpy all the time. The police searched all over and her picture was on TV too. But they never found a trace of her — or her body. Finally, Mr. Patterson applied to have her declared dead. Everybody said it was so he could collect the insurance."

My stomach felt like it had hit the floor. I looked at Kyle. "Are you thinking what I'm thinking?"

"Don't say it," Kyle answered grimly. "Maybe it's not that. Maybe he just hid something of hers in there and she wants us to have it."

"And maybe I'm really Britney Spears," I said. "Seriously, Kyle...what should we do?"

Kyle put down his empty milk glass and leaned back. "Well, we could forget all about it and..."

We both watched, horrified, as his glass tipped over and started to roll across the table. I grabbed it as it reached the edge and carefully set it upright.

Then, I looked at Kyle.

"I don't think that's an option," I said. Goosebumps had begun to spread up my legs and arms.

He nodded. "Well, then," he said, "we could tell Mom and Dad that we think there's a ghost under the carpet in the den."

We both stared at the glass. It began to rock back and forth.

"Yeah," I said quickly, "we could do that. But they'll never take us seriously. Maybe we should just check it out ourselves."

Again, we both zeroed in on the glass. It quit moving and sat perfectly still, just like a glass is supposed to.

Now I was sure I was on the right track.

"Look, Kyle." I was getting pretty excited. The words just came tumbling out. "You know how Grandma hates us to leave when we visit. Mom and Dad won't be home for hours."

"So?" Kyle eyed me suspiciously.

"So, it's the best chance we're likely to get for a while. Let's just do it!"

Kyle looked at me hard, the way he does when I surprise him. "You're serious, aren't you?"

"You scared?" I asked. I stopped talking and waited. I know how to deal with Kyle. He stared at the floor, his face twisted into a thoughtful frown.

Suddenly, he pushed back his chair and stood up.

"Okay, let's go. We better do it right now 'cause if I think about it for five minutes, I'm going to decide that we're both crazy."

As we grabbed the rocking chair and carried it into the living room, Kyle said, "You know there's no basement under this wing of the house, Liz. There might be nothing under here but dirt."

"We'll know soon enough, then, won't we?" I said, heading back into the den.

In ten minutes, the room was empty except for the new carpet.

Kyle and I got to work with a crowbar and a claw hammer. Once we'd rolled up the carpet, the floor boards lay exposed.

"See?" I said, pointing to the boards that had lifted again. "See how they're loose. Dad really nailed them down, too."

My voice echoed in the empty room. With every step we took, the floor creaked. A little light came in from the living room, but most of the den was in shadow.

Kyle wedged the crowbar under one of the loose boards and leaned on it. I grabbed the hammer and pitched in. As we pried the nails out of the old dry timber, they seemed to groan.

Kyle was breathing hard and I'd broken into a sweat by the time we'd freed all four of the loose boards. We knelt beside them, reluctant to take the next step.

Kyle's voice trembled a little as he said, "Liz, we don't have to do this, you know."

I looked at him, my heart pounding. "Yes, we do."

Kyle just nodded.

My hands shook as we lifted the boards and laid them aside. We stood at opposite ends of the long, rectangular hole we'd made in the floor, staring into blackness.

"Wh...what do you see?" I couldn't believe my voice sounded so small.

"Nothing," said Kyle. "It's too dark down there. Hand me the flashlight."

I couldn't believe what I said next. "No way. This was my idea."

I knelt beside the hole, peered in and flipped the switch on the flashlight. Close to my face, a skeletal hand reached out.

I screamed and jumped to my feet. Kyle had been leaning over my shoulder and we both fell in a tangled heap. The flashlight rolled across the floor and came to rest at the edge of the hole.

The thin beam of light revealed a skeleton. Its right hand lay across its chest, palm up, as if it had been pushing against the floorboards.

Everything happened pretty fast after that. Mom

and Dad came home to find police cars in the driveway. Lieutenant Volpe from the homicide squad was interviewing me and Kyle when they came racing into the living room.

The sight of the police cars in the driveway already had Mom and Dad in a pretty bad state. The sight of Mrs. Patterson under the den didn't help them feel better.

We spent the night at the Holiday Inn, compliments of the police. It took them a full day to finish at the house. We got a spiffy new carpet, too. The old one was carted away as evidence.

Mom and Dad heard the whole story and Mrs. Patterson finally got a decent burial. Dad had no problem going back to the house, but it took Mom a while to feel comfortable again. She kept asking me if I felt anything strange. I told her I didn't.

Which wasn't the whole truth. I don't feel anything strange, but I do feel something. Sometimes, when I'm in the den, the rocking chair starts swaying, just a bit. It's as if there's someone in it, someone who is, I'm sure, smiling. At one time, Mrs. Patterson couldn't leave. Now I don't think she wants to. I think she likes it here.

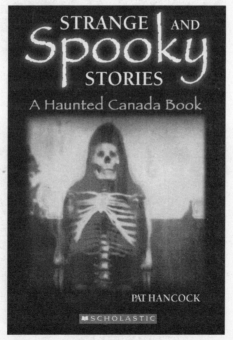

HAUNTED CANADA
True Ghost Stories

This collection of chilling true ghost stories from all across Canada will send shivers down your spine. From poltergeists who terrorize hunters in a remote cabin to a man who gets frightened to death in a graveyard, prepare yourself to be haunted!

Winner of the Diamond Willow Award

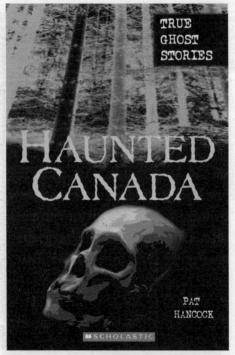

ISBN 0-7791-1410-8